IVAN!

IVAN!

A POUND DOG'S
VIEW ON
LIFE, LOVE, AND LEASHES

Tim McHugh

TURNER

Turner Publishing Company

200 4th Avenue North • Suite 950
Nashville, Tennessee 37219

445 Park Avenue • 9th Floor
New York, NY 10022

www.turnerpublishing.com

Ivan!: A Pound Dog's View on Life, Love, and Leashes

The views and opinions expressed in this book are those of the author
and do not necessarily reflect the views and opinions of the publisher.

This memoir is written from the perspective of a dog; therefore, the
sequence of events provided herein should not be construed as being
chronologically accurate.

Cover design by Mike Penticost
Art direction by Gina Binkley

Library of Congress Cataloging-in-Publication Data

McHugh, Tim, 1960-
Ivan! : a pound dog's view on life, love, and leashes / Tim McHugh.
   p. cm.
ISBN 978-1-59652-831-4
I. Title.
PS3613.C5336I93 2011
813'.6--dc22

                        2011015167

Printed in the United States of America

11 12 13 14 15 16 17—0 9 8 7 6 5 4 3 2 1

To Kristina, Casey, Morgan, and Avery

"He wa'n't no common dog . . ."
~ MARK TWAIN

acknowledgments

The process of writing a book from a dog's perspective created, on occasion, a minor identity crisis for me, though living in Ivan's mind for a while did help me see the world in a more optimistic light. Seeing the people that I've known and loved through Ivan's eyes has also deepened my appreciation and gratitude to all who have played a role both in his life as well as mine. More than a few thanks are in order here.

I'd like to first thank my son Casey for his tireless role in brainstorming titles for this book, and Morgan for the peals of laughter shaking our house as some of these chapters were read aloud. Thank you as well my dear Kristina for helping remember the stories surrounding Ivan as well as for being my first and primary reader. I also want to thank you for accepting my momentary lapses of sanity as necessary conditions for completion of this book and ultimately for convincing me to go to the Humane Society of Skagit Valley to take a look at a very unusual dog. Our lives have never been the same.

I've known for a long time that having a great book does not necessarily translate to an author's success. Having an excellent literary agent is every bit as important, so I extend my deepest appreciation and thanks to my stellar agent and dear friend Diane Gedymin for bringing this story to fruition and finding Ivan a second home, and to Charles Cantrell for introducing us in the first place. Diane, your passion, guidance, quirky sense of humor, and steely determination has made all of the difference. I know this was more than a book for you and I am so grateful to know you both personally and professionally.

I'd like to extend a sincere thanks to Todd Bottorff, publisher of Turner Publishing whose editorial and personal feedback helped bring this story to a new level. I'm humbled at your belief in this book and grateful at your willingness to take on a new writer like myself. Many thanks as well to the rest of the Turner staff for your passion and excitement surrounding *Ivan*.

I'd like to acknowledge and thank all members of my immediate as well as extended families along with all of the characters who have appeared in various places in the book as well as in Ivan's life. Though there are too many to name here, please know that you have all contributed to this story in ways you will never know. Without you, there would be no book.

Both Ivan and I thank all of the good folks at Northshore Veterinary Clinic for their boundless love, compassion, and dedication to all animals that come through their doors. Your love and support has made such a difference in our lives.

Finally, Ivan and I extend our deepest gratitude and thanks to all animal rescue organizations everywhere for their heroic, tireless, and selfless work on behalf of all animals.

introdogtion

My name is Ivan. I'm a one-eyed, three-legged pound dog with a lumpy head and an underbite, as well as a sideways snaggletooth that frequently gets caught on garments and stuff. I don't know what kind of a dog I am, and apparently nobody else does either. When I was a puppy, everyone said, "That dog looks like a Malamute that got his head stepped on." As I grew, people started seeing a little Australian shepherd and Bernese mountain dog. As I grew larger, I started hearing things like alligator, grizzly bear, gargoyle, and tyrannosaurus rex.

I was on a walk once when someone we met on the way said, "Hey, that dog looks like Nick Nolte!" Since I don't watch television and rarely attend movies, I'm not sure who Nick Nolte is except that he's probably a famous person. Everyone was laughing so I laughed too.

You might wonder why I'm writing my life story. Well, part of the reason is that I want some people to rethink the expression, "It's a dog's life." I'm living proof that life can be very good, no matter what you look like or how badly it starts off.

If you're looking for a thousand-page memoir, you shouldn't be looking here—the fact is, a dog's life is much shorter than a person's. In fact, most dogs (only because they're lazy by nature) would write their memoirs in a single sentence: "Today I got up, went outside, went back inside, got fed, laid down, received some petting, went outside again, was tied up, barked at strange noises, was untied, raided the garbage when no one was looking, was scolded and forgiven, was taken for a walk, got fed, laid down, got petted some more, and was put to bed." Multiply this by three thousand and there you have the typical dog's life. My life hasn't been so typical, and neither am I.

an original is born

Like most puppies, I was born to a single mother. Rumor had it that my father was a sleek brute with a fearsome lower jaw and feral eyes. Some even suggested that he was a young grizzly bear, while others, a one-eyed gorilla. Of course I never believed such urban-myth nonsense—clearly he was a dog of some sort, but of what sort I'll never know.

As with all homeless male dogs with their canine-hood intact, he was content to follow his nose and deepest physical instincts wherever they led him, spreading his genes and irresponsibility throughout rural Skagit Valley's alleys, barns, and the dark rainy streets of Mt. Vernon. Eventually that brought him in contact with a certain semi-homeless female, and the rest, as they say, is history.

I have only vague fleeting memories of my first weeks, except I'll always remember how lovely and highly unusual looking my mother was, with skunk-like markings on her face, and expressive, loving, big brown eyes. I try to forget one particular instance when a fierce male (allegedly my dear old dad) invaded the old shack where we were living. Shrieks, growls, and an awful barking punctured the tranquility of our little nest. A fearsome set of eyes seemed to be searching for one pup in particular.

Suddenly I felt the squishy slavering of his jaws as they slid over my snout before finding a firm grip, then a searing, blinding, electric pain shooting through my jaws and head. The stench of his rotten breath overwhelmed me as he shook me by the head as if trying to kill me.

Then, just as he got me away from the litter, there was a new round of shrieking and barking, only this time it was his screams of pain. Mom's rage-filled snarling drowned out his cries, and I can only guess where she bit him. By the sound of those squeals, it must have been a very sensitive area, and I do recall his howls turning to whimpers that grew fainter and fainter as he hobbled away. First lesson? Never underestimate the power of a mother.

the cosmic goddess of love

For the next week or so following the brutal attack, my mother licked my wounds, and I bathed contentedly in her attention. Although my left eye was destroyed, I recovered, and we puppies grew, nourished by the sweetest milk a dog ever knew.

"Look here! Puppies!" a man's voice boomed one day. I don't think he saw me under the straw at the bottom of the pile because the next thing I remember is my head being crushed with an unbelievably great weight. He must have been stepping on me! It felt like my whole lower jaw was being squeezed from my head, and that's all I remember.

It was also the last I ever saw of Mom.

When I awoke there were bright lights all around me, and I was in a cage with one of my sisters and several other dogs

I'd never seen, as well as some food. This was my first experience with solid food, and I had to fight for every scrap.

Some dogs are optimists. They see a bowl of food as half full. Others are pessimists—for them the bowl is half empty. Later on, after my immersion in Russian literature, I would learn that I was more of a visionary—I picture a completely empty bowl and always ensure that this materializes as quickly as possible. In some circles, if you take the time to savor the taste of food, you go hungry. I never learned otherwise.

I heard that I'd been rescued, but that confused me. How is having your head stepped on while being yanked away from your family being rescued? Apparently this place I was staying was going to find a new home for me, but I also heard that not all dogs were desirable enough to be adopted, and that some were put to sleep. Sleep? This was the last thing on a puppy's mind! One thing was for sure—I missed my mom!

I liked the people who took care of me though, and they seemed to like me too. Every time they'd look at me, they'd laugh. "Look at that face," they'd say. "What do you think happened to him?" Of course I couldn't explain that to them, but I was glad to make them happy. It feels good to make people laugh—sometimes. I only hoped my appearance wouldn't work against me.

"A face only a mother could love," one woman said, and I think she really meant it. "He looks like a deformed skunk!" another boy shrieked. It's the way people say things that matters, and laughter can hurt or gladden. Either way, when people laughed at me, I'd often get a little testy and was overwhelmed with this desire to bite them. Mind you, I wasn't actually mad, nor would I bite out of meanness. It's just that all the laughing somehow made me frisky.

One day the woman who would forever change my life arrived, and after noticing me, she couldn't stop laughing. I just fell to the ground staring at her with my big brown eye, my heart pounding so hard I thought it might burst from my chest. She had the most radiant face I'd ever seen. She was . . . my Cosmic Goddess of Love!

There she was, a brunette with flowing, rich hair spilling over her shoulders, and hazel eyes that sang with intelligence, laughter, and vigor. Now, I've never been a fan of Victorian literature, and that period of cultural decadence is only comparable to the one in which we now live, but she was a stunning masterpiece of beauty that immediately reminded me of Waterhouse's first *Ophelia* in 1889 depicting a stunning, long-haired maiden staring longingly past the artist—with one difference: unlike the melancholy, tight-lipped maiden, my goddess couldn't stop smiling. Yes, that's what I said! She couldn't and wouldn't stop smiling—at *me!* In that moment, I no longer missed my mother. In fact, the thought of never seeing my real mother again vanished as my goddess now became my new mother, and was now the mother of all mothers! I would gladly and proudly let her take care of me forever!

She was with a couple of kids who yelled a lot, and one even drooled kind of like me, so of course I liked them both at first sight. They were very excited to see me too. It was almost as if they knew me, but she—she was the one who swept my heart away. Then my goddess did something that no visitor had done before: she lifted me from the cage. And as soon as I fell into her arms, I squirmed up her neck, plastering her face with a million rapid licks of my tongue. She shrieked with surprise, then giggled and held me tight. I knew we were meant to be.

We walked around the building and I trotted proudly before her, trying to act like I was already her dog. Every time I looked up at her and those kids, my goddess would giggle. She kept talking to me and laughing, and I knew it was because of my face. She even said, "I think I have to take you home." I remember her commenting on how fuzzy I was and how funny my underbite was. We spent what seemed like an eternity of bliss together, and I could almost feel my eye tearing up. Then something terrible happened—worse than being chomped by my own father and flattened under someone's boot: she took me back to my cage and abandoned me.

heartbreak hotel

She left me! I'd never in my short life been in such torment. I had never felt such betrayal. Here I was, tasting the sweetness of my first hope, coming to believe that I'd been saved, and now she'd left me! I hardly slept that night, and I almost attacked a puppy that squirmed a little too close to me.

It was late in the next day that I had another visitor—not a goddess—just a guy with longish brown hair and a goatee. He wasn't much to look at next to my goddess, but he acted as if he was looking for me. A volunteer pulled me from the cage. I'd already learned that life is nothing but a series of disappointments and betrayals with some head squishing in between it all, so I didn't hold out much hope. Still, I couldn't muster up anything like anger toward anyone. In a way I understood. I wasn't cute like the other dogs, and most people were looking for dogs with at least two eyes and a muzzle that didn't resemble that of an alligator.

When this man took me in his arms, he was laughing, and I'm sorry to say this, but I wasn't as kindly disposed as I had been toward my goddess. I slipped into my frisky mode and nipped him on the cheek. He put me down. I thought I'd blown it and he was going to take me back to the cage, but instead he beckoned me, laughing a little more as we wandered around the building.

For the first time, I noticed my feet. They were big and rather clumsy, and as I ran I saw out of the back of my eye this fuzzy, snakelike creature sneaking up behind me. I turned and unleashed my fury on it, growling and snapping, and yet it just eluded my jaws as I chased it in circles. The guy laughed even harder. Odd sense of humor! This snakelike creature would follow me for countless weeks and years ahead, but I was never destined to catch it.

As we rounded the building, he picked me up and buried his face in my soft chest. I wanted to bite him hard, but I'm no fool. Instead I licked his face. I had already let go of a happily-ever-after life with my goddess and was perfectly willing to go with this seemingly kind gentleman. Yes, that fickle female may live to regret her decision forever; this guy would do just fine. Yeah, the two of us would get along very well, baching it wherever he saw fit.

Then the same terrible thing occurred that had happened the day before—he brought me back to my cage and abandoned me. I had fallen for it—again!

Hey, I squealed. Don't leave me here! If you don't adopt me, somebody's going to take me to The Room From Which No Dog Ever Returns. It will be on your conscience. Evidently he didn't hear me, but he did smile sadly at me, as I remember. I heard him talking to the volunteer for some time before he left, and it seemed to be about me. I refused to hope for anything more and sank yet again into a dark despair.

The next day, someone came and opened my cage, lifting me into the air and hustling me off toward the room I'd come to fear. This was it. All hope had vanished. I was set, trembling, on a cold metal table, and out came the needles. I cried as she stuck me, expecting this to be the beginning of some horrible end. Then, suddenly, she brought me back and there I was in my cage again, confused. Dogs and pups barked and whined around me as the usual parade of visitors came breezing past, but I just lay there under a leaden cloud of despair. No more would I trust that my dark imprisonment would end. No more would I question why I was there and for what end I was created. No, I would just live out what time I had in the cage, knowing at least that I'd get one meal a day to fight over and a little exercise walk from time to time. I was doomed.

perfection

Just when I thought all was lost, everything changed. It started with the door opening and a familiar female voice greeting my ears. I heard the rustling of papers and low voices. An eternity later and there she was, yet I didn't dare fully believe that she'd come back for me. Could it be my goddess had returned? In spite of myself, I felt my tail thumping the ground so hard it hurt.

Her big brown eyes smiled with relief and I remember her saying something like, "Thank God you're still here! You are perfect! Just the dog we were looking for. We hardly slept last night thinking about you!"

Seriously? I'm perfect? You were looking for a lumpy-headed, one-eyed dog with an underbite and a snaggletooth? That was all it took. I lunged against the cage door, setting off a deafening chorus of the barking and yelping of the other dogs. I had to bite some of them (sorry guys) to clear a path as the door opened. Now I was being lifted up into those same loving arms, and this time I licked her face and kissed it a billion times. She didn't want me *despite* my appearance. She didn't choose me because she felt sorry for me.

I.

Was.

Perfect!

lucky dog

Her name was Kristina. Kristeeeeenaaaa! I wanted to howl her name like a hound. Already I'd learned a huge lesson that I wanted to tell all the dogs I met at the Humane Society: you've got to hold fast to your dreams no matter the odds! If you hang in there, someone will rescue you and things will turn out better than you'd hoped.

When we finally arrived at her house, there was a very familiar smell about it that I couldn't quite place. The "house" was really a small cabin in the woods with a big maple tree hanging over it. Suddenly the door opened and I realized the source of the scent. It was that guy who had taken me for a walk at the pound. I felt a little guilty since I had forgotten all about him once Kristina showed up to rescue me.

Now I saw that not only would I be living with him and

Kristina, but also with a big black dog I came to later know as Sid. I trotted in like I owned the place, gave Sid a quick sniff and immediately knew he wouldn't be much of a threat to me. I did want to bite him just to show him who was boss, but I decided to hold off a little so as not to make a bad impression.

The guy's name was Tim. He picked me up, I wiggled a little as he kissed me, and then he put me down. A water bowl was placed before me and I slurped a whole bunch of it. Apparently it was pouring from my misaligned jaws and I made quite a mess, but no one seemed to mind too much. Then I saw a food bowl hovering in the air, attached to Kristina's hand. Instinctively I rocketed upwards, propelled by my two powerful back legs, and I'm embarrassed to say that my head caught the bottom of the bowl, blasting thousands of pellets into the air, bouncing off the ceiling, walls, and floor.

After pausing for an embarrassed moment before realizing that their laughter was a sign that I wasn't in trouble, I began quickly trotting around wolfing up the pellets, only pausing for a moment or two to growl at the old black fart who struggled to his feet to join in the feast. (To make sure this would never happen again, they would later train me to sit still in front of my food bowl until they said, "Okay." I also think they did this because they enjoyed watching the drool pour like a waterfall from my underbite onto the floor. Sadists!)

Afterwards, I plopped down on the floor and I think I fell asleep. This was not a bad beginning to a new life—even a pound dog could figure that out.

ivan the good

The next day they started calling me Ivan, and I think it had something to do with my underbite and snaggletooth but I wasn't absolutely certain at the time.

My family talks about Tolstoy a lot and his relentless pursuit of truth, but I didn't make the connection. Tolstoy insisted that everything a person says and believes must agree with human reason lest we be led astray. He has been a huge influence on our entire household, and it would stand to reason that the name Ivan came from my family's immersion in Russian arts and culture. Ivan Illych was the protagonist in Tolstoy's classic story about the slow, painful death of a government bureaucrat. There was also Ivan the Terrible, who lived long before Tolstoy, and I've heard he was a very awful human being, though truth be told, it's impossible for me to imagine any awful person, except for the one who cut my testicles off. Even that woman smiled and talked soothingly to me as she snipped away my doghood. I think that Ivan the Terrible was made up, sort of like the Big Bad Wolf.

Maybe my family named me after Ivan the Great, who united a large chunk of previously autonomous Russian provinces while freeing the country from the cruel Mongols. Maybe not. As a one-eyed mongrel, I could only unite a group of people howling at me with laughter as they pointed at my face.

Since people tell me that, in spite of how funny looking I am, I'm a good dog, let's just say that I'm Ivan the Good. I prefer to think that I was named after the Tolstoy character Ivan Illych who achieved enlightenment at the end of his life before passing out of this world. I'm not sure what enlightenment is, but I hear the word a lot around our house. I hear them say I'm enlightened. I think I'm just a dog.

new digs

I grew a lot my first year and I didn't always understand what was happening. All I knew was that every time I wolfed down a meal, I wanted more and they wouldn't give it to me. I was always hungry, and I wondered if they were trying to slowly starve me to death.

Bellingham was the name of my new town, and everywhere we went, people would pet me and laugh at my face. "What an unusual looking dog," some would say. Sometimes on walks, I would follow interesting people, and without thinking, try to go home with them. It wasn't driven by lack of love for my family as much as by curiosity about the world around me. I heard Tim comment more than once that I was a free spirit wanderer who had no loyalty—I would go home with anyone. He didn't seem bothered by it as much as amused.

I suppose during those days he was right, but there was so much to see and smell and dig for! Truthfully, in spite of my carefree nature, I was proud to have such wonderful people to take care of me, and I enjoyed following behind Sid on our walks. Something about the way he walked triggered this irresistible urge to attack, which I often did in my furious puppy sort of way, snarling and biting him on his tail and ears. He'd turn and snap at me but his ancient jaws were no match for my quickness and he'd end up sitting on his butt needing help to get up again. This always earned me a scolding.

Sometimes Sid even deigned to play with me—and maybe, just maybe, he felt like a puppy again for a minute or two. If I'd felt like I could take on a bear a few weeks ago, I now felt that there was no mammal on Earth that was a fair match for me. But perhaps I learned a bit about where to draw the line between dog play and power plays from my wise old mentor Sid.

snowflakes and teardrops

As the winter progressed, Sid seemed to be sleeping more and more. When he was awake, he'd shiver, no matter how warm it was, and often Kristina washed him with warm water in the wheelbarrow. I'm sure Sid appreciated, as did I, what a mother she was to us, but when she would grab me and soap me up in the wheelbarrow, I didn't like that at all. Talk about making me frisky—there was nothing like being given a bath to elicit a bite, though I never bit too hard.

One day the phone rang, and Kristina answered. Suddenly tears were raining from her eyes, and I came to learn that one of the kids who was with her when she first found me at the Humane Society had died. He (and the other child who had been with her on that day) had lived in a group home for children with autism, which is where she worked. I wanted to lick her tears away and fix her broken heart, but they just kept coming. I now learned that my goddess was truly special, and not just to me.

My first snowfall was a December blizzard that dumped three feet. They took me outside and tossed me into a drift where, in a panic, I began burrowing through the icy pillows, looking for my cabin. I followed the sound of their laughter, and when I popped out, I was furious and began attacking the white twisting flakes and the cold powder that was trying to choke me. This snow lasted a week at least, and then it was gone. I knew it must have had something to do with my eating as much of it as I could.

That winter we'd go down to Chuckanut Creek, where I'd chase salmon until I was caught by Tim or Kristina. I'd also attack branches and small bushes, shaking them angrily, spraying their matter all about me as I imagined them as terrified, squealing rodents. I believed I was the ruler of all I saw.

Sid really started slowing down, and as we'd climb the hill, he'd stop to rest, sides heaving as Kristina propped him up. I was curious as to why he was so slow. Dogs should run, dart, and play. I felt sad for him that he was sick.

The spring came and a great wedding between Tim and Kristina was to be celebrated. The morning before, we all gathered on a lawn where Sid was laying. He hadn't been moving much in recent weeks and could hardly get off of his bed anymore. I remember lots of tears, especially from Kristina, and I tried to lick them from her face as best I could. Our vet took out a needle like the one used on me at the pound, and stuck him with it. I thought it was going to make him better because Sid seemed to relax. But the more he relaxed, the more people were crying. I tried to be as cute as I could to make everyone feel better. Then Sid whispered good-bye to me and I knew that he wouldn't be coming back.

The next day was a gorgeous spring wedding uniting Tim and Kristina in holy matrimony—I was the best dog. Having pictures taken was sort of exhausting, but it was worth it. They got some good ones of me. I sure wish Sid could have been there.

On the honeymoon, we all headed toward a remote little island off of the west coast of Vancouver Island, but shortly after leaving home, the van started smelling funny and we had to pull over on the side of the road while Tim said words I'd never heard before. After spending hours in a garage, we made it to our destination and, once there, I smelled my first wolf. That's the thing about us canines—we have powerful instincts and senses. I could smell a poodle in a living room a mile away with all the doors shut. I could hear a cat drinking from a mud puddle a block away. I could smell a squirrel a hundred feet up a tree.

Yeah, in those days I was pretty good, and for the first time, we were a family.

abandonment revisited

After the honeymoon, just when I thought life was bliss, Ma and Pa decided to move into another house and they abandoned me—again!

They left me in the cabin as they brought a load of their stuff to the new place. Here I was in an empty building, no furniture, no nothing. I could hear the sound of birds outside, but inside I was in turmoil. It probably didn't help that I had munched a few green apples from a tree at our new place, and had slurped a bunch of water from a bucket with a mop in it that tasted like soap. I was in an absolute panic, ready to burst, when I noticed the ladder they'd use to climb into the loft.

To this day I don't know how, but I actually scrambled up the ladder rung by rung until I'd reached the top. Oh great,

Ivan, I thought once I was up there. What are you going to do now? There was no way I could get down. I felt I was being punished, but why I couldn't know. Maybe now that they were married, they didn't want me around anymore. I was done for.

Hours later, I heard laughter and then the door opened, and there they were. "Ivan?" I heard someone say. "Ivan?" The voice sounded panicked.

I'm up here, I tried to say. Suddenly a shocked face popped up at eye level.

"How did you get up here?" Tim choked. "This is impossible."

I wagged my tail weakly and did my best to apologize for the mess I'd made. He didn't know that I had doubted their love. Instead of scolding me though, he took me in his arms and began apologizing to me. For years I would hear this story told about their one-eyed ladder-climbing puppy.

Soon, we were living in our new house. It's not as difficult as one might think for dogs to move, though I must admit it took some time for me to adjust, which included establishing the perimeters of my new territory. Thus far, I'd concluded that I was the luckiest dog on Earth—maybe even the universe. I also learned that just because you are abandoned once, doesn't mean it will happen again.

call of the wild

That autumn, I had my first close brush with disaster. It was a night of blistering wind and rain when I first heard them calling up on the ridge. Tim was reading a book called *Into the Wild* that documented Chris McCandless's ill-fated adventure in the Alaskan wilderness. I was lying at his feet when I became aware of a presence outside. Coyotes. Something about the whimpers and howls drew me to the door, and I whimpered a little myself. Kristina, not hearing them, restlessly got out of bed to open the door.

I can't explain what triggers a dog's chase instinct, but I will say this: there has never been a dog in all of history (toy poodles don't count) that wouldn't bolt toward another dog, let alone a group of dogs, that had disrespected his territory.

I shot off the porch as about ten coyotes scattered into

the blackberries, shrieking and yipping. Just because these coyotes were my cousins was no reason I would tolerate their arrogance and gall. It's true that the night rain almost blinded my eye, but as I've told you, my sense of smell was unsurpassed.

I flew after them, snarling, alive in my puppy power. At the edge of our property, there is a swampy area that gives way to a wooded ridge that climbs gently upward. I'd gone up there a few times in the day, but night was a different story. I'd always smelled danger up there and vowed to never venture there after dark. But on this night, I broke my vow.

It pains me to admit this, but even on dry ground, I didn't exactly possess the speed of a greyhound—in the mud, it was even worse. As I churned through the muck toward the ridge I seemed to be following one coyote that was moving a little slower than the others. Something about this stirred a primal suspicion. I slowed down, and as I did, the coyote in front of me stopped as if waiting for me. Meanwhile, the others yipped and howled tauntingly, and I could almost hear ancient voices in my heart warning me to go no closer.

The barking was maddening, and I ignored my instincts. I growled furiously, daring to believe that I would lay to waste dozens of these scrawny fiends if necessary. It was then I heard another noise, a sort of high-pitched screaming that sounded strangely familiar. It was coming from behind me. *"Ivan! You come now!"* I turned and slowly plodded back through the swamp toward their calls. I looked back. The coyotes were gone.

When I saw Tim, he was standing in the pelting, twisting rain, shirtless in his boxer shorts, legs bleeding from the blackberry thorns. Kristina was almost crying, and I knew I was in big trouble by the way they were yelling. As I drew closer they suddenly saw me and fairly collapsed in the mud and rain with relief, which surprised me. At first I had no idea why they were afraid for me. Then I learned that coyotes often try to lure dogs away from their yards in order to kill and eat them. I couldn't believe that coyotes actually eat their own cousins, and I scoffed a little at the thought of these ruffians giving me too much trouble, but nonetheless it was a little startling to consider that I had been led into a trap. I couldn't really imagine that I'd have tasted very good, but this incident brought me face to face with another huge lesson: even if members of your own species betray you, people never will. At least not my people, whom I will be hereafter referring to as my family. I could clearly see now that it was their nature to rescue. Of course this led me to ask a bigger question: Just what was *my* nature, and for what purpose had I been born?

nature or nurture?

What is an animal's nature? Is it simply physical survival, and perpetuation of the life of its particular species? Or do we have an inherent need for something more? Is our individuality something innate and irrespective of the environment in which we live, or are we blank slates, destined to be programmed and shaped by greater minds?

Dogs around the world have been asking such questions since time began, and because perpetuating my bloodlines was not an option for me or any other pound dog, my young mind naturally drifted to philosophical questions like these. I could already sense that it was my nature to wander as a solitary canine, but there had to be more than this. What was at the root of this nature business? Through a series of often painful lessons in the coming years, I was destined to find out.

fender bender

This happened early in my second year. Most dogs would be proud to say that they've survived getting hit by a car. For me, it's a little embarrassing. While it's true that I was involved in a car accident that involved my running out into a busy roadway, I didn't actually get hit by the car. No, Ivan, in his rush to defend his dear Kristina, smashed into the driver's side door of a moving car while running at full speed after a deer. The deer of course got away unscathed though the same couldn't be said of me.

This occurred when I was taking Kristina out for one of our runs. I remember stopping and staring intently into the brush and Kristina, believing I needed to do some dog business, took me off the leash for a moment before telling me to go. I went all right—right into the brush, snarling at the creature within. The deer shot out onto the sidewalk and directly into traffic on Bill McDonald Parkway, narrowly avoiding a bus and a car. Me? Like I said, I wasn't so lucky. Evidently I put quite a dent in the Volvo's side door as I slammed into it, almost giving the driver a heart attack. I also cut my head and lip pretty good, while breaking my foot in the process. Though I didn't lose any teeth, my family says this accident may have also increased the gap in my underbite. The broken foot came courtesy of the car's back tire rolling over it. I was in a cast for weeks.

I learned from this that it is my nature to chase ungulates impulsively, and to act without thought of consequences.

pavlov is not the boss of me

Whosoever would be a man must be a nonconformist."
When those timeless words were spoken by the great
transcendentalist Ralph Waldo Emerson, he must have been
thinking of someone like me. Emerson theorized that each
of us is governed by a cosmic, all-seeing, transparent eyeball.
I wonder if, in his mind, there was a celestial underbite that
went along with that all-seeing eyeball!

I was never sent to obedience school, thanks to my family's mistrust of authority and belief in the principles of reason governing one's cognitive development. This allowed me
to blossom in my own individuality.

I also learned through my visits to the dog park amidst
the whispers in the canine world that many people actually
train their dogs using a system of rewards and punishments

and stimulus-response, very similar to the methods used in human obedience schools, where most people send their children. These methods were refined and espoused by Skinner and Pavlov (no relation to Tolstoy). Some of these techniques were applied to me as well, but here is the point at which I must be totally forthcoming about dogs—you can teach us to do anything for a snack reward, but it doesn't mean we've succumbed to the dictates of laboratory scientists wearing white robes.

Case-in-point: My good buddy Diane (Kristina's best friend who was like a nanny to me) taught me a "go-through" trick where I would be commanded to go through a person's legs counterclockwise in the shape of a figure eight and, upon completion, I would be given a snack. I was well aware that I was being manipulated into learning this through subtle coercion, but I also rationally weighed the consequences of not doing the trick—no trick, no snack. At face value, this would appear to validate the reasoning behind the experiment, but because I saw myself as endowed with a free will and the ability to shape my destiny through a series of personal choices, the experiment took on a completely different dimension.

As one who believes in the Socratic method as the most vital ingredient in a dog's cognitive development (people talk—dog barks back questions after a rational intellectual engagement using the principles of logic and reason as prescribed by Aristotle), I would rationally evaluate each situation in which I was asked to participate in this game. Was the treat worth the effort? Was I being respected as a sentient, autonomous individual? Might I decline based on a simple act of will related to my mood and temperament for that particular day? Might I at any time alter the nature of the figure eight based on my own choice?

I have come to the conclusion that the fact that I would salivate 100 percent of the time I was given the command was complete coincidence. One time this trick almost caused a disaster. I was out for a walk showing off my goddess on Vendor's Row at the local university when an elderly woman in high heels walked out of the campus bank with a treat in hand. "What a cute dog," she said.

Of course I took this as permission to lunge for her legs. In the process, I caught my head and teeth in her skirt. She screamed as I plowed through her, forcing her to hop backwards in the pattern of a perfect figure eight. She did an impressive job considering the heels she was wearing. I blame this unfortunate event on my snaggletooth and the shape of my head. In the end, I got the treat, while everyone but she had a good laugh—the best positive reinforcement a dog could ever want.

a confession

It's easy for a dog to say the cat did it, but my buddy Boris is truly almost always the guilty party when it comes to swiping food off the table. Yes, it's true that once or twice when I was really little I scrambled up onto the kitchen counter and raided the compost container, but after bloating to the point of almost exploding, I don't behave in such a manner anymore. As far as taking perfectly good food from our family, it's always Boris. Every dog knows that cats cannot be trusted.

It's true that both he and I have battled eating disorders most of our lives, and while I've considered counseling for this, I did not steal the three bricks of exotic cheese from the table once when we were left alone. I swear the cat did it, but to this day nobody believes me. A few words about Boris (named after a famous Russian, but I'm not sure which one)—he's a splotchy, grayish white cat who is truly in denial about his overeating. (In the winter he gets so fat he lodges himself in the cat door and it takes a couple of us to free him.) Don't get me wrong: I like Boris, but he's a schmoozer of the worst kind. All cats are clever, but Boris . . . well, let's just say he's downright calculating.

My family had just finished preparing a cheese and cracker dish for a potluck when they had to run out to the store for something. As soon as the door closed, Boris looked back and forth between me and the top of the table, purring loudly. "Shall we?"

"No," I replied. "They feed us and take care of us and we mustn't take from them."

"It's not 'taking,'" he hissed. "It's sharing the wealth." He then confessed his weakness for extra sharp cheddar, and that was it. Up on the table he went, knocking the plate to the floor as the cheese bricks went flying. I do admit that, once the cheese hit the floor, I wolfed it down, but I did not initiate the action that led to the consumption of this food. I learned that I had a special place in my heart for gouda cheese, and chuckled to myself as I imagined Boris hereafter calling me Ivan the Gouda.

Boris never forgave me for swiping the cheese from him, even though I explained to him that it was my nature to teach him a lesson about morals and ethics, even though I put my own integrity at risk. Isn't that what love is all about?

not all who wander are lost

Imagine, for a moment, Nick Nolte's face on milk cartons throughout America. Of course I can't since I've never seen him, but regardless, how long do you think it would be before he or any famous person like him was found? Probably not that long, and the same would have been true for me except that at first, believe it or not, I did not want to be found, as I'd been swept away by another goddess of rare beauty and I'm ashamed to say that it wasn't Kristina.

This first disappearance all started with a double mocha. Actually, it may have been a triple Americano—I can't remember Kristina's preference. All I remember is this sweet girl named Jessica working Kristina's favorite espresso stand who would give me not one dog treat but two. The way she flashed her pearly white teeth in my direction before handing me the biscuits made me want to leap from the car and into her arms! Some might call it puppy love, but I honestly believe that I came to love her in the way Tolstoy describes ideal love between males and females in his brilliant yet controversial work, *The Kreutzer Sonata*. It was a love that transcended the physical—pure and divine in origin.

The truth was I couldn't get Jessica out of my mind. Every couple of days when Kristina would get within a few blocks of the stand, my nose would moisten and I'd start to salivate, but again I remind you that this had nothing at all to do with classical conditioning. It was my choice to drool all over my blanket in the back of the car. It's also important to realize that we canines have an incredible sense of geography, as portrayed in *The Incredible Journey*. I could have found her stand with my one eye blindfolded, but as it turns out, this wasn't necessary.

One innocuous afternoon during my second winter season after my broken foot had healed from my collision with the driver's door of that Volvo, I smelled her. It was just a faint whiff, mind you, but the fact that I was two miles away from her stand made no difference. I've already told you how keen was my sense of smell, but this surprised even me. Amidst all the odors of squirrels, dogs, poop, pee, cats, people, deer, bears, cougars, and skunks wafting about on the unseen breezes, I smelled her. Jessica. Her sweet essence was distinct from the millions of other females including Kristina. As if in a trance I rose from the grass, realizing that I had no chain or rope to restrain me. Indeed, someone had forgotten to put my collar on me. For a moment, I was no longer Ivan the Good— I was a nothing, a nameless canine, wanderer of the earth, seeker of wisdom, love, purity, and meat snacks.

My family was inside the house having lunch with

friends and had no idea, nor did I, that my legs suddenly, as if through a force of their own will, would begin taking me through dank woods, swamps, condo developments, roads, and trails. I was going to her, and she would carry me the rest of the way to my divine destiny.

the idiot

I have no idea how long it took me to arrive at her stand. I remember little of the trip, actually. The only thing I remember is the sound of many horns telling me that perhaps I was wandering out into traffic. Find her I did, however. She was just getting ready to leave and was closing up shop.

"Ivan," she said, her voice sounding like tinkling angelic bells. "What are you doing here?"

I've come to bring you everlasting bliss, Jessica my true love. Take me with you anywhere. I care not what lies ahead, only that we're finally together. I stood before her, trembling, gazing up at her with my big brown eye, a strand of drool falling from my jaw as I anticipated the impending treat.

"Ivan," she giggled. "Where is your collar?"

Collar, what collar? And who is this Ivan but a name

assigned to me by the well-meaning caretakers who have yet to know me for who I truly am—a canine god-steed come hither for my truest and sweetest love, Jessica.

For a moment, I was Dante standing in Paradise with Beatrice beckoning me to cross the babbling River Lethe, destined to wash away all memory of darkness and sin. Once I crossed, there would be no going back.

She pulled a dog biscuit from her purse and I took it oh so gently from her slender fingers. I chewed and swallowed it quietly, stifling a belch. Another biscuit was produced and this time I snatched it from her fingers, startling her. I wolfed it down.

"Ivan," she exclaimed, giggling with surprise, "look at your teeth! You are the silliest looking dog I've ever seen and I bet your owners are worried sick about you."

Owners? I thought. I am owned by no one and will answer to no one but you. Take me, Jessica, and I will be yours forevermore.

Take me she did. I climbed into the back of her car, and we drove as I anticipated my new life with her.

As we pulled down a long driveway, the first thing I remember was the sound of barking. Lots of barking. The car came to a halt, the door opened, and there were suddenly five sets of eyes peering into the car. Holy wolf excrement! What were they doing here? She scolded them, chiding them to get away from the car. I was mad with jealousy, and the mane on my shoulders stiffened like a porcupine. A black lab dared to sniff me.

"Stay your distance, lowly beast," I whispered to the lab. "I will rip the heart from your chest and hang it on my snaggletooth should you dare challenge me!" I bared my underbite and then trotted around the yard and began marking. This was too much for the black lab and suddenly we were locked to each other in a blaze of snarling fury. Of course I would swear that the lab was the one who started the fight, but since I was more or less a stray, I knew I lacked credibility. Jessica scolded me, which told me I'd made a lousy impression. She led me to the backyard, where I was forced to spend the night chained to the fence while the others were brought inside.

I learned that you can win the fight, but victory often has a bitter price. It was clearly my nature to fight other male dogs who challenged me, but I could see that following this instinct led to trouble. Fyodor Dostoyevsky, an amazing writer from Russia, once wrote a book called *The Idiot*. I haven't read it, but the title suggests that it was probably written about someone like me.

ivan the fool

That night I hardly slept at all, but instead contemplated my situation to the best of my ability. In spite of my emotional attachment to Jessica, I reasoned that life would be difficult if not impossible with five other dogs. It was only night one and she had tied me up outside, not that I could blame her. As I'd allowed myself to be swept away in a careless fantasy, I hadn't even considered what other players might be involved in this unfolding melodrama. Mind you, ever since those early days at the Humane Society, I had grown to hate drama.

As the dark hours progressed, my heart grew more leaden and I began considering my old life and what I'd had before I'd so flippantly wandered off. Shelter, love, security, and people who loved me was what I'd known in my former life.

Right now all I knew was that everything was uncertain, including my return home given my lack of identification. As much as I loved Jessica, the other dogs were extremely annoying and they made me question her taste in dogs, which logically made me question her judgment in other matters.

As I considered the benefits of my former life, I now felt something I'd rarely known before—guilt. I began to get very sad. The sadder I got, the less Jessica meant to me. By morning, I was missing my family with all of my heart and wanted to go home. As it turned out, that wouldn't matter, and I would have to spend an entire day with my fate hanging in the balance.

There was no word on even the possibility of me going home and there I stayed, chained to the back of the fence. Jessica did take me for one walk, as did a male whom I'd never seen before. I couldn't have known that, back home, Kristina and Tim were sick with worry about me, putting up posters with my face all over Bellingham. A couple of days after I went missing, Kristina stopped by Jessica's espresso stand to buy a mocha and have a poster put up. Imagine her surprise when Jessica said, "Oh! Ivan's at my house!"

The rest was history. Shortly after this encounter, Kristina was covering me in kisses and squeezing me so hard I swear I felt my ribs crack. Wow! I wanted to tell Jessica that this is how it could have been with us, but as I climbed into the car, my heart turned back to Kristina. All I cared about now was the fact that I was going home.

This incident raised many more questions than it answered. Was it my nature to wander away from home? Was it my nature to fight? Was it still my nature to impulsively chase large ungulates into traffic? I didn't yet have any answers, though I did learn that loyalty, friendship, and true love were things I probably didn't deserve. I was mystified that they were given so freely to me by my family despite the foolishness of my ways. Speaking of foolishness, Tolstoy also wrote a story about another fellow, "Ivan the Fool." No comment.

amelia

Amelia. I was with Kristina when we first saw her, lying in a patch of weeds on Interstate 5 just north of Ferndale. Kristina had just gotten off of her shift at the group home where she worked, and had taken me with her, as the kids there were so fond of me. I was a little sore from all the petting and pulling of my hair, and one very excited kid kept drooling on me and yelling "da" which was a little annoying, but I'd tolerated it pretty well. He had been with Kristina the first day I saw her at the Humane Society, as the kids loved to go on these sorts of outings, and I suspected he'd had something to do with my being rescued.

Anyway, we were just heading home when Kristina squealed, "There's Amelia," and suddenly we were pulling over on the side of the freeway.

That's when I noticed a golden retriever heavy with pups, sides heaving and tongue hanging from her mouth, just lying there staring at us with a goofy grin plastered on her face. When I say heavy with pups, I mean she was ready to pop at any moment. Here she was, abandoned!

How did Kristina know her name? Had we just found Amelia Earhart? If she was that Amelia, I knew she had flown way off course. I couldn't remember whether or not Amelia Earhart was a golden retriever, but I suspected not. Then I wondered if this was the St. Amelia from Lobbes, or even the infamous Amelia Vega Polanco from the Dominican Republic who'd been crowned Miss Universe. A few glances over this swollen retriever eliminated these possibilities. The question, however, remained.

Though her breed is not my favorite, I did feel sorry for her, and was glad that Kristina, with no prompting from me, helped her into the back of the van. Then we were on our way home.

a rocky start

A minute hadn't even passed after Amelia entered our house when disaster struck. Tim had inherited a parakeet named George from a former music manager and while he wasn't exactly fond of domesticated birds, this one was pretty sweet. He and Kristina let it fly loose in the house, and the bird seemed to instinctively know to avoid flying into windows which told me it was pretty smart. It also knew how to stay away from Boris who, at least on the surface, acted indifferent about it, but I didn't trust him at all. I was not allowed to even so much as look at that bird, and I didn't. I thought it odd that a bird was allowed to fly free in our house, but after a while you get used to things like getting pooped on and stuff. Tim had grown quite fond of that bird.

Here's what I remember: After pulling into the driveway,

Kristina opened the side door of the van and we both jumped out and ran around the yard, sniffing and peeing. Kristina had a bag of groceries in her arms and was struggling at the door to find the right key. She called to us and we ran up to the door. All I could think of was that I needed to get to my food dish before this new stranger, lest there be a surprise scrap or something. The door opened, and in we ran, which startled George, causing him to flutter off the top of our bookcase, across the room, and directly into a window. Once he hit the glass, his wings battered helplessly against it as he quickly lost elevation, and that was all it took.

In a surprising demonstration of speed and agility, Amelia launched herself from the door and over the couch, and with her jaws snapping like a steel trap, she crunched the bird in an explosion of feathers. It was over that quickly.

"Amelia!" Kristina yelled, dropping her bag of groceries as the dog stared stupidly back, the poor bird's tail feathers poking out of her mouth. "Bad dog!" She pulled Amelia roughly off the couch and the dog hung its head, the bird still in her mouth. I was horrified! Even Boris looked on with unmistakable tension in his face. Amelia dropped the bird and it fell to the floor, wet and quivering. Amelia stared at Kristina and then began wagging her tail, trying to nudge her head under Kristina's hand for a reassuring pat which is, by the way, one of the most irritating habits in some dogs. The only time I ever do this is when I need a scratch behind the ears, as my self-esteem is high enough that I don't need constant validation. I was sad because I didn't think my family would understand that Amelia was living according to her nature, just as George was living according to his. Really, the death of

George wasn't as tragic as it looked. I could probably explain Amelia's nature better than my own.

That night when Tim got home, he wasn't exactly thrilled at the news of losing his bird, especially from a bird dog that he'd known nothing about. "I loved that bird," was all he kept saying. As I suspected though, his anger at losing his bird was more than tempered by his love of Kristina, and within the hour she not only had him forgetting how angry he was over his loss, he was actually out in our shed, working with her to prepare a place for Amelia to give birth to her pups. He'd expressed his dismay at having five or six little "Amelias" running around our house and property, but Kristina insisted she would find all the puppies homes when they were born. Amelia was to live in our house until the pups came, and that was okay by me but not so much for Tim.

I later came to learn that the name Amelia came from a children's book series called Amelia Bedelia, written by a woman who loved hats. Though I knew the killing of George was simply Amelia's nature at work within her, I still wanted to tell this dog how important it is that we live up to and honor the goodness of our names. In spite of her quirks, it was fun having another dog around, especially a female. While she wasn't exactly spry, she didn't mind me chewing on her face and we played pretty well together. Our favorite game was tug-of-war. Once together, we were able to turn Kristina's merino wool sock into a four-foot masterpiece. She was not amused!

However, I soon came to realize that, personality-wise, Amelia wouldn't fit into our household. Boris hated her hyperactive tail-thumping and constant desire to be petted, as revealed by his angry, half-shut eyes and flattened ears. She would gum him relentlessly to the point where he was sticky and wet, and I knew she just wanted to get him outside for a good chase. Boris mostly tolerated her constant slobbering on him better than most cats (I'll give him that), but I empathized with his disgust. Amelia was, in short, a dork.

It wasn't a week after welcoming Amelia into our home that the shed was filled with eight squirming black pups. Three died shortly after, and we were down to five. We were now the focus of the entire neighborhood—everyone was coming over to see the new litter, and I'd hear people talking amongst themselves about what a special person Kristina was for rescuing Amelia after she'd been abandoned.

I tried to imagine the person who'd abandoned her, but I couldn't. I'd met only nice people in my life so far, and this behavior seemed so contrary to everything I'd come to know about people. Maybe the person was sick or dying; clearly not in his or her right mind. I wondered if this person had regrets and later came back to rescue Amelia, only to find her gone. I'd like to believe that this was the case.

Over the next few weeks, the pups grew quickly and, as they did, I found myself letting them crawl all over me, biting me everywhere. It occurred to me that this is how grandfathers must feel, and it made my heart sing. At eight weeks they were gradually given away as people lined up for them, mostly friends of my family. One was chosen by our neighbors, so at least I'd have that one to play with, but I can't deny feeling sad about it all. Things quieted down until finally, only Amelia remained. I can't say we were very close, as any mother about to give birth is going to be preoccupied, but time spent together in any capacity is likely to create bonds.

Amelia wasn't really my type, and as you'll see in the following chapter, even if she were, given the status of my malehood it wouldn't have mattered, as I was never destined to know the joys of fatherhood. Finally, she was gone, adopted by a single woman with the same hair color as Amelia who was apparently lonely and in need of an abandoned female dog. I remembered my hopeless days at the Humane Society and was now coming to believe that dogs should just expect their luck to change, as being abandoned is simply a stage of life we're all destined to experience. I was happy they found each other, and in the coming years Amelia and I would play together from time to time.

hey you! out of the gene pool!

I know for a fact that my family never entered me in an ugly dog contest primarily because they were afraid that I'd win. Bless their hearts. Consequently, I've never experienced the excitement of *Best in Show*. This is, of course, my favorite movie, and I bark and drool hysterically every time I watch it. I truly wish there was a *Best in Show* for pound dogs.

Once when I was just minding my own business down at the off-leash dog park, I overheard a conversation between a Norfolk terrier, and an English bulldog. Mind you, I've got great admiration for purebreds and as you'll later learn, my family had some wonderful ones, but the conversation taking place between these two particular dogs was appalling. My first instinct was to run over to them and establish myself as the supreme alpha male, but I decided to stay put and listen. Over the next few minutes, I wanted to hang my head in shame. Their words hit home as I realized European aristocracy, replete with its class system, still exerted some influence on our vast melting pot. I pondered my lot as a muzhik—a lowly peasant who apparently had no place among such affluent pedigree—while they continued.

"You should see my papers," the English bulldog said. "I got first place last week and got to ride in the front seat of our Hummer on the way home."

"Your papers?" asked the Norfolk terrier. "How much did your owners pay for you?"

"You know, I'm not sure, but I think it was a lot," said the bulldog.

"My owners paid five thousand dollars for me," boasted the terrier. "The breeder says that I'm the perfect dog." Then he grimaced for a brief moment and his body shuddered as if in pain. He sighed and lamented, "I sure wish they'd stop feeding me Dungeness crab cakes with prawns and garlic sauce every day. Wreaks havoc on the lower gastrointestinal tract, if you know what I mean."

"Lucky you," said the bulldog. "My owners want me to live for at least fifteen years, and are trying out this awful pureed vegan diet. What I would do for the taste of Dungeness crab, you lucky dog. I don't mind some of the vegan food, but green super-food does get rather old after a while. Maybe if my colonoscopy tests come back clear they'll ease up a little. Now that you mention it, I do wonder how much they paid for me."

The terrier said in a condescending fashion, "I'm sure it was at least a thousand dollars."

"Oh, it was more than that," said the bulldog. "I'm sure it was."

"Twelve-hundred dollars? Depends on the breeder of course. You know who it was?"

"The papers suggest that it was someone reputable!"

"Could be fifteen-hundred, then. That's not too shabby. You know a greyhound can go for 10k these days?"

"Yeah, but they don't live that long," said the bulldog. "Don't get me wrong, I mean, I'd like to know what it feels like to be worth that much, but you know they do have issues."

"We all have issues, I suppose," said the terrier, suddenly noticing me as if for the first time. "Say, what is that thing over there?" He was now pointing his nose in my direction, ears up.

"That one-eyed thing?"

"Yeah, how much do you think he's worth?" They both laughed, and I could feel my hackles rising as I gave them my meanest one-eyed glare.

"Who does he think he is, staring at us?" scoffed the bull-dog. "What a freak! Should we attack?"

"I'm not bred for that purpose," whined the terrier. "I'll bark and such, but I don't want to mess up my claws. If you are so inclined, then by all means, go ahead."

That was it! I'd had enough of their snobbery and insults. I noticed their owners were engaged in conversation some distance away and momentarily not paying attention, and since I love a challenge, I trotted over and, in moments, we were all cautiously squaring off.

"How much are you worth?" yipped the terrier, standing cautiously off to the side.

"What do you mean how much am I worth?" I asked. "My family says I'm priceless."

"Of what stock do you hearken from?" asked the bulldog, unimpressed.

"Stock? I don't know. Of what stock are you?" The question was still confusing me.

"I'm not sure either," said the bulldog, "but my owners paid possibly two thousand dollars for me. How much did your owners pay for you?"

"I'm not sure," I said, thinking hard. Had they asked me ten years later after all the vet bills were added up, I might have given that 10k greyhound a run for his money, but at this point in life, I was relatively cheap.

"Who's your breeder?" asked the terrier. "That might give us some indication."

"My parents?" I asked, as they both burst into fits of snarling coughs and I realized they were laughing. "I don't know . . . I was claimed from the Humane Society."

"The Humane Society?" chirped the terrier. "Then you were free!"

"No," I insisted. "I think with all the fees, it cost my family around a hundred dollars."

"A hundred dollars?" Suddenly the little terrier was shrieking like a poodle on steroids. Soon, I realized there was laughter echoing all over the dog park, and as I looked around, a few of the dogs had stopped what they were doing and were staring at me. Suddenly, I just wanted to go home. I looked for Kristina and saw her all the way across the park talking to another woman, her back to me, and I realized that she probably didn't hear the commotion.

Now the bulldog was directly in front of me, staring me down, and I bared my underbite as I realized that a fight was likely unavoidable. He bared his underbite, too, and there we were.

"Leave the park now, lowly muzhik!" He growled. "Go back to your Baltic slum."

"I am Ivan," I growled. "This is my park, and I'm not going anywhere."

We continued circling slowly and I knew once I made my move, it would have to be quick. I didn't need any more head trauma in my life, and bulldog jaws are strong. It had all come down to this, a battle to the death for sole possession of the earth. I sensed a stationary object off to my lower right on my blind side and slowly lifted my leg to lay claim to what was mine. Suddenly there was screaming and barking.

"Patches!" yelled a woman as she stormed up to us. I turned and saw that I had soaked the Norfolk terrier, and the little dog was shrieking in unintelligible gibberish. "What kind of a freak of nature are you?" she hissed before snatching her little dog and storming off. I would have attempted an answer, but sensed it was more of a rhetorical question than anything. Besides, any dog that ventures to my blind side is taking a risk. Now the bulldog retreated a few steps, confused by this sudden turn of events just as a woman across the park was calling him. He looked at me, shook his head with disgust, and snorted in my direction before turning and trotting away.

"That's right, run away, coward," I growled. "Ivan rules this park and don't you forget it!" I turned back to my personal business and as I did so, an Oscar Wilde quote from

Lady Windermere's Fan came to mind: "What is a cynic? A dog who knows the price of everything and the value of nothing." I actually think he might have mistakenly referred to people, but I'm absolutely sure the statement was meant for certain dogs. I wanted to bark that quote at all of them, but sensed the futility. I came to the conclusion that dogs who talk like that, be they pound dogs or purebreds, are shameful, and I'd be embarrassed if people could actually hear them. I'm just glad that humans aren't so shallow!

on civility

When I consider the behavior of a few of my contemporaries, I fear the influence they might have on people. Humans talk using the principles of reason and logic; dogs snarl and bark at each other, forever defending their turf, always reacting to the slightest perception of disrespect. I'm obviously as guilty as any dog of this even though, as you've already learned, my family has been coaching me on the principles of love and reason. Love and reason seem to abandon me whenever a dog challenges my dignity.

In fact, much of the barking and snarling you hear at a dog park is probably the result of philosophical disagreements, many of which are not grounded in reason. The next time you see two males fighting, it might just be that Nietzsche-loving nihilistic rottweiler who simply can't tolerate the mastiff's bland, Kantian existentialism. Of course, a Tolstoy-loving, one-eyed mongrel has no excuse for ever fighting back, but I'll be the first to admit that the spirit is willing though the body is weak, as my nature has taught me. I could explain more, but I think you get it by now. Humans are much more dignified, no doubt.

my town

Bellingham, as you already know, is my town. Of course I know a lot of other dogs live here, and Bellingham also has an inordinate number of cats who might claim it as their own, but let me reiterate: Bellingham is my town. Did I tell you that Bellingham is my town?

Okay, at least the south side that we all call Fairhaven is mine even though I've marked every shrub from Fairhaven Park to Lake Padden, and from Marine Park to Squalicum Harbor. 21st and Donovan? I chased my first cat besides Boris there. Chuckanut Ridge? I got my picture in the paper as we protested a huge housing development that was planned, right square in the middle of the most amazing greenbelt in all of the city. Meridian and Squalicum? I beat up a rottweiler. Vendor's Row? I was the poster dog for a campus-wide protest to keep it from being turned into a strip mall. I got my picture in the paper then too!

Yeah, this is my town and Bellinghamsters are all family to me, even if they're not quite as odd looking as I. Generally, I don't like crowds and cities, but Bellingham is a little different. Bellingham is like one big family, and it seems like everywhere I go, strangers call me by name.

"Hi, Ivan! What are you up to today?" they'll cheerfully ask, and it seems like almost everyone is glad to see me. I like the attention, but also grow a little weary of it at times, due to the fact that I can hardly remember everyone's names. I know how Bono must feel, but I'm not sure people offer him treats and snacks like they do me. Poor guy.

my kind of canine

There are a few kinds of dogs I have great admiration for, and some who grate on my nerves, but I reserve my greatest admiration for wolves, though I will say that I did have a particular fondness for a huge purebred sheepdog named Dustin I met at Fairhaven Park who loved to show me his belly! He was a humble brute who relished life like I did. Besides toy poodles and dogs that are programmed to retrieve, dogs that bark too much and dogs that chase cars really do irritate me. First allow me to address the dogs that bark too much.

Most dogs that are accused of barking at nothing are in fact barking at something. It may be a twig snapping in the woods a mile off, or a car door slamming down the street. Some dogs twist the meaning of Descartes' philosophy on reality, "I think, therefore I am" into "I am, therefore I bark." I must admit that I've been guilty of this at times, but not often. When I bark, there's always a reason behind it even though that reason is not always clear to me.

As for the dogs that chase cars? They actually believe that cars are a form of big game not unlike a moose, deer, or caribou. Many of these dogs weed themselves out of the gene pool, but for every dog that ends up squished under the wheels of a car or truck, there are ten more born. Now, I know you're probably thinking about my collision with that Volvo. I might remind you that I was chasing a deer and not a car. It was my poor aim and judgment that led to this embarrassing accident, but not my intention to chase something that was clearly not a form of big game.

The same types of dogs that bark and chase cars also bark at (and sometimes chase) people. This is, in my opinion, a cardinal sin. People are great! Would a dog bark at God? I think not! Those that bark at people are doing almost the same thing, in my opinion. I've even heard of dogs attacking, injuring, and sometimes killing people. This is the work of the Devil himself! If I was ever to see a dog doing this to a person, God help him! I would fight him to the death to defend any person against such evil.

Now let's turn our attention to the stick dog. It's not just the redundancy of their actions with the predictable outcome—throw the stick, bring it back, throw the stick, bring it back—that gets me; it's the effort involved for nothing but, in the end, exhaustion. It's even worse when there's water involved.

I will swim if I have to, but not to fetch. On a hot day I will especially take advantage of standing water, but overall, I avoid getting wet unless it's coming from a rainstorm. I don't mind that at all. If I have to swim across a river when going hiking, I don't mind that either, at least I didn't when I had four legs, but now things are a little different.

my inner wolf

After my run-in with those two dogs I told you about, I stopped going to the off-leash park as much, even though there's no place I'd ever been with a wider array of incredible odors emanating from the grasses and bushes. I'd finally figured out that these parks are created by social engineers to promote uniformity in the dog world, but as we've recently seen, I've never been accepted there anyway.

I once punctured a purebred cocker spaniel's ear by accidentally stepping on it during a skirmish there, and its owners accused me of biting it! They were pretty upset about it, and I came to the conclusion that city parks are just too much trouble. The wild woods are a much better place for a dog to get in touch with his inner wolf.

turn the other tooth

I know this is a touchy subject for many people, but I'll say straight up that while I'm not exactly sure what the Creator looks like, the fact that I'm a one-eyed dog with an underbite and snaggletooth shows a great sense of humor. (This missing leg comes later.) Tolstoy claimed that reason is our only means to knowing truth, and what cannot agree with reason must not be called truth. Apparently, this eliminates much of what people and dogs believe, but I'm in no position to critique human metaphysics in the way others might be. I am, however, in a position to critique canine metaphysics.

I believe that dogs were put on Earth to guide humans on the path from darkness to light. Even Tolstoy said that we were all at various places on this path, and our purpose is to help each other follow the law of Love as we disentangle ourselves from the world of strife, suffering, poodles, and cats.

In the spirit of truth, I must make a confession. I do not dislike little dogs, nor do I hate cats. May I remind you that Boris is still my buddy? The fact is, really tiny dogs and cats in general terrify me. My bristling and curiosity are only superficial ways that I deal with the irrational fear that sweeps over me whenever I'm in their presence. I don't know what to do with them. Should I sniff them? Should I bite first and bark questions later? Should I try to play with them? Should I run? My first instinct is to always sniff and then bolt.

I've heard of the wars throughout history and the cruelty of man, but if I were to formulate my beliefs based on my experience alone, I would say that people are closer to divine than dogs. In all of my life I've never met a bad person. Sure, I've heard about them, and all the great thinkers have mentioned them often. Through the dispensing of food, shelter, water, and companionship to those less fortunate, they have at least shown themselves as divine to me. Don't get me wrong, I've met some very strange people with odd behavior, and those who own mean dogs should certainly be called into question. However, in my opinion, everyone deserves to be cut a lot of slack. Everyone needs to be understood. Everyone needs to just be.

I've been a great admirer of Christ and have learned that his followers try to imitate him by taking care of the sick, unwanted, one-eyed, underbitten, lumpy-headed, and three-legged. Gandhi was a wonderful man, though his vegetarian sensibilities are a little rigid for a meat-eating pound dog like me. In spite of my desire to eat large amounts of anything ranging from potatoes to broccoli, meat is the best, and I couldn't pretend otherwise.

My religion has required me to trot my bark. I knew I had a long way to go in spite of how much I'd come to love people. I still fought male dogs, though I knew it wasn't right. "Turn the other tooth" or "Turn a blind eye" were the mottos I tried to live by as I strove to extinguish the lowly beast within me.

walden revisited

While it's true that there was a lot of talking done in our house, there was also a lot of action. The day I came home to my family I found myself living in a cabin built by Tim out of wood and materials salvaged from construction sites. So inspired was he by Thoreau's transcendentalism, he left his job teaching high school English to pursue a life of nonmaterialistic idealism, music, basketball, and wilderness travel. His family was concerned about the unconventional life he'd chosen, having left a job that would be the envy of many people, but he'd come to realize he needed a break from life in an institution. A lot of his contemporaries wanted to study Thoreau and transcendentalism in books; Tim wanted to live it!

I'd heard him say he'd never built anything, but always

said that if people wait around to ask for permission to try things they've never done, nobody would ever do anything worthwhile. He says that if you don't know how to do something, find someone who does. Tim didn't even own any property, but that didn't stop him from building his dream house.

At a potluck he met a woman who was building her own house. They got to talking, and he learned that she lived on the edge of town in an area with lots of big trees, few houses, and a stunning pond. Being English majors, they had a lot to talk about, and soon she was offering a piece of her land for him to build a cabin on in exchange for him helping her finish her house and complete some other projects. This was Tim's first immersion in the bartering community that had been growing in Bellingham for some time, and he accepted the offer. Between living in a tent and a camper on her property, he helped work on her place, and applied his newfound carpentry skills to the building of his own place, also under the guidance of other carpenter friends and Kristina, who helped immeasurably.

Down in the woods overlooking a stunning pond that could be seen through the trees, Tim built his cabin at almost no cost and spent the next six years bartering, playing music, and working odd jobs so he could read and write while enjoying a waterfront view! This must have been what it was like for Thoreau at Walden Pond, and I'm sure he would have been proud! Eventually, Tim was joined by Kristina, Sid, and then, me!

It was also during this time that Tim was invited by Sarah James of the Gwich'in Tribe in Alaska to tour the Yukon River and the Arctic National Wildlife Refuge. Upon his return from Alaska, he was invited to powwows and concerts up and down the West Coast, as saving the world had become a full-time job.

Shortly after my arrival, I got a great taste of this life-style—I would spend days at a time in the cabin listening to him write songs, type away, or just lose himself in books. This is where he got hooked on writers like Tolstoy. It was like he'd found a friend who truly understood his mind. I understood his mind too. He just didn't know it.

Now we were all living the dream! We'd pile into the car and travel to gigs all over the place, and while I would occasionally have to wait outside, mostly I'd be able to attend the shows, cheering on my most favorite band in the world—the Lost Poets! They did have a mascot—a punk-rock style pygmy goat with a pink Mohawk, but I always liked to believe that I was most important.

rock me, baby

As you probably gathered, I love music. My family plays a lot of music, and I sort of drool and hum along quietly when nobody's paying attention. I listen to all kinds of recorded music as long as it's good. Neil Young, The Beatles, Pink Floyd, (especially the song "Dogs" off of the album *Animals*), Nick Drake, Beethoven, Pavarotti, The Moody Blues, The Boss (I love Bruce Springsteen's underbite!)—you name it—if it's played or sung well and with passion, I'll probably love it. I'll be straight up with you though—Johnny Cash is one of my greatest heroes. I'll even take it a step further—I feel that Folsom Prison Blues was written for me. It helps me get over those lonely days at the Humane Society. Johnny Cash speaks to my heart in a way that no other does.

Having said that, I do have a few other heroes. One hero

of mine is of course my buddy Tim. He often plays and sings for me when it's late at night and everyone else is asleep. There is, however, a singer I really need to tell you about—a guy named Greg Brown. Greg is a friend of mine, too. Any guy who comes up with a song called "Slow Food" is a friend of mine. The song describes home cooking with gravy drippings and all the things I love that take time. It has been noted that I suck my food like a vacuum cleaner, but in spite of the speed with which I eat, I do have great appreciation for food cooked slow, seasoned in its own juices. Never judge a dog by the way he eats.

Actually, I've never seen Greg in concert, though I was in the car outside one of his shows during my second year of life. After the show we were all invited to this party where lots of people hung out with him, talking to him and stuff. He looked rather bored and uncomfortable being in such a large social scene where people were trying hard to impress him, and after a little while, excused himself to go outside. I was out there waiting. I trotted over to give him a quick sniff.

"Look at that face," he mumbled to me in his deep baritone as he took my head in his hands, staring into my eye. "What happened to you?" Suddenly his hands were patting me and rubbing my head. He was totally lit up, as if he was as much a fan of me as I was of his. "What's his name?"

"Ivan," Tim said.

"Ivan," the legendary folk singer said, kneeling down to pet me. My second favorite singer of all time was roughing me up and loving me for who I was! "You have a beautiful face, Ivan. Your teeth are perfect."

I trembled with excitement; someone other than my own

family found me beautiful! My teeth were perfect! Artists and musicians are very kind and appreciate beauty in ways that many others don't.

If I could have talked, I would have asked him to sing me his song, "Slow Food." Since I couldn't talk, I growled happily as he petted me, talking about how much I reminded him of his old dog Blizzard back in Iowa. Greg talked of trout stories, and camping adventures in the Northwest. This was one of the most starstruck days of my young life. We said good-bye after a while, and I wanted to tell him how much I hoped our paths would cross again and that maybe we might all go fishing sometime. Lifelong friendships can be made on the spur of the moment, even if those same friends are never seen or heard from again.

gone fishin'

Pat. Pat was Tim's dad, and he was my buddy since we understood each other in ways that nobody else could. He was a heavyset, balding man with a bulbous nose broken countless times in his younger days from getting jumped on his way to Catholic school and playing football with leather helmets and no face guards. He was a cheerful man who was ever-loyal to his wife, Bernice, a first-generation Lithuanian woman of bajorai nobility who secretly filled my mouth with table scraps during meals.

Actually, both she and Pat would do this, though Pat would often yell the words, "Ivan, get out of the kitchen!" right after giving me a scrap. This always confused me a little, but I was okay with it. They both came to visit regularly. Bernice's favorite topic of discussion was religion, and she often tried to engage everyone in a morals debate that usually turned passionate, if not heated. (If Lithuanians are anything like their Russian contemporaries, they can get pretty wound up talking about such things.)

Pat was very private about religious matters, but not about other things. He loved to sing and tell stories and didn't really care what others believed as long as they were good-hearted human beings. He was a lot like me—he never met a person he didn't like. He also loved a good dark ale, and a shot of Irish whiskey from time to time. His easygoing nature was all the more impressive given that he was in constant pain. Not many people noticed, or perhaps they'd just grown accustomed to it over the years, but I saw it. I could feel the heaviness of his legs and feet as they struck the floor and could tell that it was very difficult for him to even rise from a chair.

I came to learn it was the result of rheumatoid arthritis that had come on when he was a young man. Apparently the combination of working in a smelter and being an offensive lineman in high school led to this. I've heard stories of my ancestors pulling sleds over vicious terrain, and could somehow relate to this. Pat never once complained, and every time Tim would ask him if he needed help, Pat would wave him off, saying, "I'm fine!"

When Pat had his way, the conversation usually turned to fishing or sports. I'm personally not that much of a sports fan, though for some reason I do like basketball. At least I liked the funny way Tim yelled at the television screen when the Sonics were in the playoffs. But fishing? I love fishing! Pat always told great fish stories, and on this day, Pat reminded

Tim of a giant trout he had once almost caught when we all went fishing together. As he finished the story, I just about choked on my tongue, aghast at what he had said!

This day had found us at our usual spot on the local river, a sandy beach by a pool that was easy to walk to since Pat didn't do very well on uneven ground. Often Tim would wander away out of sight, always trying to catch the "big" one. Now, back to my choking. One reason I choked is because Pat had the nerve to say that it was my fault that this monster trout he hooked got away! He told Tim how he'd battled the fish for over ten minutes and that he had even called out to him to no avail. He described the fish tugging violently on his pole and thrashing in the water and finally when he got the mighty fish to the beach, I pounced on it, snapping the line off while it swam off! Yes, he blamed me! I couldn't believe it!

I'm embarrassed to admit that I did go in the water, but it wasn't after any fish that Pat had on his line. I just like to snorkel sometimes, and am fascinated with trying to catch minnows in the shallows. What really happened was that Pat tangled his line on a submerged log and was standing next to me yelling words that I won't dare repeat before finally snapping his line off in disgust. Then he looked at me, and I saw his wry Irish smile as a thought came to him, realizing there were no other witnesses but myself.

By the time Tim returned from downstream, the log had become a fish that was at least two feet long, and he told the story so emphatically that even I almost believed him. I learned that day how legends and myths were born!

Pat loved telling this story for some reason, and I was always forced to listen to it. I also came to notice that all of

Pat's fish stories took place when Tim was out of sight and I was the only witness. I wanted to tell him, "Tolstoy would be ashamed of you!" Then again, Leo might forgive Pat for exaggerating. After all, Tolstoy was quite a storyteller himself.

a different sort of stray

When I was a pup of no more than two years, my family brought home another stray. I didn't know he was a stray at the time, but only later deduced this from stories that were told. This stray was not a lost or runaway dog, but a lost person. The man they brought home had gotten lost intentionally.

Adam was his name and he was a solid person with a voice as smooth as a collie's back. He took to me right away, laughing and teasing me about my face, petting me roughly around the head, and he seemed to just laugh and laugh. It was like I'd known him forever! When he laughed, his smile seemed to light up the room, though it also revealed a beautiful gap in his front teeth. "Hey," I wanted to say. "You're not exactly one to talk about funny faces!" Truth be told, though, he had a beautiful smile in spite of lacking an underbite.

Adam, I soon learned, was a stray artist who drew and painted beautiful pictures, leaving a trail of them as he wandered around the country. He said he was looking for his piece of heaven and had big dreams of one day finding it. He told us that when he got sad, he'd get some paper out of his pack and draw a beautiful house by a lake or river and try to imagine himself sitting inside staring out at the beauty. His dream was to sell his art, and when he saved enough money he would have a dentist fix his teeth before moving to the house in his pictures, where he'd spend the rest of his life unless of course he happened to fall in love with a woman and start a family. I wanted to tell him that his teeth were fine compared to the state of mine, and that if he fixed them, it might change him. We really understood each other, and I was glad to welcome him into our family, at least for the time being.

Eventually, he got an apartment in town where he stayed for a couple of years as he worked to establish himself. He'd often come over and cook us fried chicken, corn bread, and red beans with ham hocks. Boy, was he a good cook and did he ever take care of me! Unlike my family, he seemed to understand my true food requirements, and every time he was cooking, he'd slip me tasty pieces of chicken fresh out of the pan. But, the room he was living in eventually grew too small for his spirit, and he explained to us that there were people in town who wanted him to go away because they didn't like his skin color which, to this day, I cannot understand.

the human condition

It was a sleeting, wind-battered evening in November. We were all sitting around the kitchen table playing a game called Scrabble and I was on the floor waiting for scraps to fall. Scrabble is a really interesting game to watch people play. It usually starts out calm, but then everybody gets excited while Kristina and her sister Colleen (who also happens to be my personal vet) take turns throwing water at Tim. Sometimes the board goes flying with the wooden pieces filling the air. Scrabble in our family is almost a contact sport, and though they don't let me play, I do tend to bark a lot when things get rowdy. (It's important to note that they never threw water at Pat out of respect for elders, even though Pat won almost every time, and he did so in devious fashion. For example, if he suspected that someone had a *q*, he would hold on to every letter *u* if possible.)

This night, Pat and Bernice were up, and Pat was winning as usual. Though there was much laughter, I sensed sadness in the air underneath the pleasant chattering, and knew it had to do with Pat. He seemed even more unsteady on his feet these days, and I'd heard that he was on kidney dialysis. I could feel that he was hanging on to life for everyone else's sake.

Apparently sometimes you live longer than you even want to when you know others are counting on you. I was glad to have him around. Finally when the game was over, Pat struggled to his feet but before he was upright, he lost his balance and went over backwards, slamming into the kitchen counter and on to the floor.

"Call 911!" someone yelled frantically.

"I'm fine," Pat insisted, wheezing and then laughing. "Just let me lay for a minute."

Tim picked up the phone and Pat yelled at him which made me cower a little. "Don't call!" Then he laughed again. "I'm okay . . . I'll be okay."

Everyone gathered around him, trying to help him up from the floor, but he was too heavy. I wanted so much to help him myself, but even though I'm strong, I'm just a dog. Finally Tim informed everyone that if Pat wouldn't let them call an ambulance, he was going to call Adam. I understood why right away—Adam was a strong, husky-chested male like me. But, unlike me, he had hands that could grab.

I heard Tim's soft voice in the other room talking with Adam on the phone, and then he was out the door. Not too much later he and Adam were both back. As Adam walked through the door I trotted over and gave him a quick sniff, and as my head pushed into his leg, his warm hands softly scratched behind my ears.

"Adam," Pat laughed from the floor, "How are ya?" Here was my Pat, lying flat on his back in a world of pain, asking others how they were doing! It was just like him!

"I'm okay," Adam said, "but you don't look so good." He paused and then smiled. "Maybe we should leave you right here! Keep you out of trouble."

"That'd be just like you, Adam," Pat wheezed. "Come on now, get me up!"

"Yes sir!" Adam mimicked his tone, and in moments he was lifting Pat to his feet and helping him over to the soft chair. Man, was he strong! Somehow having Pat sitting up made everything seem normal. Kristina cleaned the wound on his head, but it was clear that both he and Bernice would need help once they got back to Olympia, which was a three-hour drive from our house. "I'll go," Adam offered. "I got nothing else going on anyway. I'm all packed."

"What do you mean you're packed?" Tim asked.

"I gotta go."

"Why you gotta go?"

"I ain't welcome here." He looked at the hurt expressions on everybody's faces. "No, that's not what I mean. Y'all are my real family and if everyone was like you this'd be heaven. Everyone ain't like you though." He went on to tell us about Mickey, and by the time he was done, I knew that if I ever saw Mickey, he might be the first person I'd ever consider biting. Mickey hated all people who weren't white, and I imagined him to be like those two dogs I met in the dog park who asked me how much money I was worth. Since that incident I've found it best to ignore dogs and people like this, and wanted to tell Adam that he could do this too. I knew, though, that if I was to hear Mickey say the things Adam told us he'd said, I'd bite him right on the yapper. I was also so shocked at this new information—there were people in the world that weren't nice to others! As hard as I tried to get my mind around this, I couldn't!

"I best be movin' on," Adam said.

But you're welcome here! I thought. I wanted to tell him that there are probably snooty people and dogs everywhere and their opinions about the color of one's skin, the shape of one's lower jaw, or the number of eyes and legs one has shouldn't carry a lot of weight—it's what's in your heart that really counts. I wanted to tell Adam this, but being a dog, I couldn't. Besides, he showed us clearly with his kind actions what was in his heart.

"Don't you worry; I'll take care of Pat 'til he's back on his feet. Then I'll be on my way."

He slept on the couch that night, and the next morning he helped Pat and Bernice to the car, setting Pat gently in the driver's seat. Adam promised to come back to say good-bye before he moved, and then they were gone. I knew Pat would be in good hands.

Six weeks later, Adam showed up again to say good-bye. Pat was back on his feet, and was able to drive himself to his dialysis appointments without assistance. Adam had done a lot of work around the place as well—splitting fire-wood, landscaping, cleaning, and helping Pat in and out of the shower. When Pat tried to pay him, Adam refused to take any money. Then the elders lectured Adam, telling him that he'd be offending them greatly, and he wouldn't want to do that, would he? Bernice would go on and on in the following years describing what a great Christian Adam was, and how they wished he would just stay and live with them. They tried to talk him into it, but Adam would hear none of it.

When he finally came back to Bellingham to say good-bye, we tried to convince him to stay with us. He just kept saying that it was time for him to go. He left and I was sorry to say good-bye. He seemed to know me in a way that no one else did.

A couple of years later, he showed up at our house again. He brought us some new drawings and practiced reading books to the children. True to past tradition, he snuck a few extra table scraps into my mouth when no one was looking. He whispered to me that I was one of the big reasons he came back. Then he was gone. He still hadn't found a woman to marry or his piece of heaven, and I knew that this time he wasn't coming back. Adam was a dreamer like me, and I believed he would roam for the rest of his days. He taught me that you can never find yourself if you don't first allow yourself to get lost. Boy, could I relate to that.

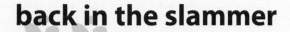

back in the slammer

Getting lost . . . I knew that wandering and getting lost was part of my nature, but this next incident is pretty hard to believe given my painful lesson with Jessica. I have to admit, though, that I did wander off one more time. This time, it wasn't inspired as much by a forbidden love as by a hungry curiosity. There was a new espresso stand just a few blocks away, and I had to see if they gave dogs treats there. I never got to find out. When I got there, instead of a treat someone in a uniform threw a tether around my neck and took me back to the place of my worst nightmares—the Humane Society.

Horrified by the nature of this bitter turn of events, I was yet again locked in a cage with a bunch of strangers, and because they were closed to the public on Sundays and Mondays, I spent a couple of the longest, noisiest days of my life there, wondering if I'd ever see my happy home again. During this time I reflected on what mattered to me the most, and my mind came back to my family—they mattered the most. If I were so lucky to be reunited with them I would never wander off again.

Lucky for me they actually did come. As I sprang to greet them, I felt joy shooting like electricity through my limbs. They greeted me and I covered them with wet kisses. Rescued again! Was there anything my family wouldn't do for a pound dog like me? The sound of my own bark was strange to me, like my voice had changed a little bit, but Colleen told me later that it was just a case of kennel cough. All that mattered now was that I was going home—again. My family's loyalty and love had no limit.

the fruits of enlightenment?

I've always loved babies and small children because they are clumsy when they are eating and since one of my most important jobs is to keep all kitchen floors clean, it's a win-win situation for everyone. After all, there's nothing worse (or better) than a messy child.

The structural makeup of my lower jaw actually helps me be more efficient in keeping floors cleared of food waste. The underbite scoops, the snaggletooth catches, and when I employ deep breathing simultaneously, the result is not dissimilar to a high-powered vacuum cleaner minus the noise.

Like I said earlier, I do eat vegetables, and when the apples are ripe on our tree, I find them a great way to alleviate the insatiable hunger I'm forced to endure. I'll eat ten to fifteen apples a day when they're in season, but my bottom line is meat. My meat is usually served in the form of dry dog food. This doesn't bother me at all. I know some dogs won't eat it unless it's wet; for me, dry works just fine. It's my nature to devour food and as you've seen, there's hardly ever enough given to satisfy me. Tolstoy wrote another story called "The Fruits of Enlightenment" (he wrote a lot—I always wonder when he had time to eat). Fasting may encourage long-term enlightenment, but I'd trade enlightenment for a good meal any day. Sorry, Leo.

new life

They say when you have kids your life changes, but I couldn't have known how true that was until it happened. At first when I heard Kristina was pregnant, I assumed she was going to have several puppies at once. It wasn't until later that I realized it was just going to be one at a time. While it was true that in the coming years both sons would be excellent sources of supplemental protein due to their clumsiness at the table, I would come to love them as more than just another food source.

First came Casey, born at home. Our midwife named Winnie (who absolutely adores me) helped us pull him out. I guess I didn't understand how unusual and special it was for a dog to be present at the birth of a human pup. It all seemed so natural to me. It was only later that I would learn that most people are born in hospitals surrounded by strangers with no dogs or cats allowed.

The new "pup" didn't even bark for the longest time. He just stared at all of us in wonder. I knew it was my divine destiny to guard him with my life. If I had already decided to never wander off again, now I was determined to live up to this.

It was somewhere during this time of new arrival that Pat, Tim, and I all went to the river to go fishing one last time. I didn't know it would be the last time, but as Tim helped Pat from the car and led him over the scorched river rocks baking in the August sun, I could see that Pat's steps were ever slower and faltering, and I thought of old Sid. It was a warm day, and I could just feel that Pat was working hard.

It seemed like we sat on the beach all afternoon, and Pat hardly tried to get up to fish, though I was quietly begging him with all of my canine heart to wade out into that current and try a few casts, to just give it a shot so things would feel normal in the universe. I would even grant him permission to make up any story he wanted about me, just to feel the sweetness of a moment in nature with all of us together, doing what we loved.

As we sat there, without thinking, Pat put his arm around me and gave me a squeeze. Then he left his arm there, and I knew the love that Tim must have felt as a little boy. Now, I'm not a hugely sentimental dog, but having Pat's arm around my shoulders was nice. I felt a love humming in his soul that was too great to be contained by this failing body of his. Pat was telling me with his gentle hands that I was his dog too. How sweet it was.

After a while, he perked up and said he wanted to fish. We stood up and Tim and I helped him step out into the current. The yellows and reds of fall shimmered against the crisp blue sky, and the clear gurgling water that swirled around our legs seemed to hold us there in one endless moment. A warm breeze wafted off the water, and I drew in a deep shuddering breath of nature's divinity, realizing that this was a moment made for me, for us. A peace I'd never known swam through my soul like a great unseen fish, and I knew that I was not just important to Tim, but to Pat as well. The moment was over far too soon. Pat was wobbling unsteadily and I noticed sweat pouring over his face from under his cap. He asked for help getting to shore, and we led him over to some big rocks where he sat down again.

Tim's eyes were wet, and I felt my eye moistening. (A lot of people don't think that dogs cry but we do, even though we are stoic.) There was a lot of talking back and forth between Pat and Tim, and what I gathered was that Pat didn't have much time left. Pat gave Tim instructions that he didn't want to hear, but I listened carefully since an elder's instructions are to be heeded. Tim was asked to take care of his mom and to handle Pat's affairs as well as assuming guardianship for Pat's youngest brother, Chuck, who was disabled and lived in another place that sounded an awful lot like the Humane Society to me.

He agreed to this, and there were long moments of silence. I wedged myself between both of them and served as a distraction, which worked, as they both began petting me and squeezing me hard. After a long time, we finally helped him to the car and drove back to Olympia.

I was learning so much—the true purpose of life is found in helping and comforting those around us who can't help themselves, keeping them on their feet as long as possible, and squeezing every drop of life out of moments like these, as they are what make us who we are. I learned that it was my nature to savor these moments and times, and to stay present in the moment.

On the way home, Pat's singing voice filled the car with old songs from Ireland, and I felt something within me change too. There was something familiar about those old songs, even though I'd never heard most of them—something that connected me to my past. For a few brief moments, the universe around me swelled and buzzed . . . everything was a little louder and a little brighter. I knew that sooner rather than later, more tears would fall.

sewing things up

As if all of this wasn't complicated enough, I should tell you that during this last stretch of Pat's life I went to the vet for my first surgery. My blind eye had shriveled like a raisin and my snaggleteeth were growing outwards and sideways like white spikes, and apparently I looked even goofier than before. I'm not sure what was causing the teeth to migrate like this, but I did learn that my eye had shriveled due to the lack of a functioning tear duct. The shriveled eye didn't bother me too much, though it was starting to itch. Everyone thought it looked weird, however.

Before, when people would first notice me, they wouldn't necessarily see that I was blind unless they looked closely. The eye was milky looking and all, but of normal shape. Once it shriveled, though, my eyelids looked like they were collapsing inward. Colleen thought it would be better taken out and the lids sewn together. There was some talk of inserting a bionic rotating laser eye that could be programmed by remote control, but luckily that didn't happen. I think that maybe they were joking about that idea.

moving on

It now seemed like every weekend we would all pile into the car and make the three-hour drive to Olympia. Tim had all but stopped trying to survive on his music, choosing to devote his energy to caring for parents and babies. Though he knows how lucky he is, I'll say it too. He is the second luckiest dog in the world besides me to have such a goddess as Kristina who fully supported the efforts to help Pat on his journey.

Once in Olympia, Tim and Kristina would clean the big old house, drive Pat to his dialysis appointments, mow the long lawn, split and haul firewood, and just visit, letting little Casey's voice fill the house with happiness. Often Tim's sister Kathleen's family would be over, and I loved all the attention they'd give me.

Having us all show up took some of the edge off of the

sadness hanging heavily in the air. We'd all watch Mariners games, and during this time I became a huge fan, if only because of play-by-play announcer Dave Niehaus screaming, "My oh my!" every time Edgar Martinez or Ken Griffey Junior belted a baseball out of the park.

We all hung on to these moments, trying hard to pretend like there was more time left than there really was. Pat would always call me to come over, and I would relish sitting next to him as he softly petted me. Kristina was swelling with another pup and we were all holding out hope that it would arrive before Pat left so he could see his growing legacy and the beautiful future he'd played such a great role in creating.

Pat had grown so tired that he mostly just sat in his rocking chair and when baseball games weren't on, he'd be singing old songs to Casey, his favorite being "The Band Played On." Somehow the title of this song seemed to be a metaphor for life—no matter what happens, we do our best, and then move on. I loved the image of Casey waltzing with a strawberry blonde, and wondered if this song was a prediction of some distant, happy future for my little pup.

Meals were served, and of course I would watch with envy as everyone ate, hoping for my usual scraps. I noticed that the amount of leftovers that were deposited in my bowl increased dramatically, and it finally occurred to me that this was because Pat wasn't eating. I knew the day I stopped eating would be a bad sign, and I felt both guilty and thankful for the added food bonus.

"Spectacular Pat!" I wanted to say. "You are dying well and I'm proud of you. Thank you for the extra scraps but mostly, thank you for the love!" I wondered if everyone else knew how hard he was working to stay with everyone. I'm sure they did, as my family seems to know just about everything worth knowing. We were all working hard in our own ways, and my job was to observe, comfort, and provide an important diversion. I rationalized the extra food as a reward for a job well done. I stayed extra-close to Pat and it was akin to lying near a woodstove, filled on a cold winter day—he radiated a certain aura that was warm and welcoming. I always slept soundly when I was near him. When nobody was in the room, he sang and snored, and I think that he was singing for me.

Then, one spring morning Pat died. The prior two weeks had been very difficult for the family, and they didn't allow me to go to the hospital, but I just hoped I'd get to see Pat once more. I know they tried to get him home to let his spirit pass under the open sky, but it didn't work out. The family had been at the hospital for days, and Kathleen's family was also there to bid Pat farewell. I loved that part of my family and just wish I saw them more often.

Even though I was home when Pat passed, the birds were singing a little louder than usual and the sun was a little brighter. I knew. I'd heard about angels, and could almost see the heavens opening with Pat's spirit being welcomed by a chorus of laughter shaking the cosmos. I knew that morning that it wasn't just Pat singing anymore. I was as happy and as sad as I'd ever been. I'd miss him greatly, while I guiltily lamented how my food rations would return to normal.

After the funeral and procession to the cemetery had passed, we lingered at the grave site, staring down at a small urn that was apparently filled with Pat's ashes. I thought it strange that such a big man, with an even bigger heart, could fit in such a tiny container. I could just imagine Pat laughing over such a silly thing.

As we stood over the open hole in the ground, staring down at the urn, Casey looked up at Tim and Kristina and asked, "Is grandpa in heaven?"

"Yes, Casey. Grandpa is in heaven," Tim replied.

"Is that heaven down there?" Casey asked, and I just wanted to howl, but felt that wouldn't be right under the circumstances.

another pup is born

Morgan arrived a few weeks after Pat's death, and by the racket he raised, I just knew that he was going to be a big-hearted singer like Pat. Again, Kristina birthed at home with our midwife Winnie, and of course I was invited in the room. As we all absorbed the glow and majesty of this little baby's presence, I suddenly felt Pat's warmth as certainly as if he were snoring in the chair next to me. When Tim raised Morgan in the air, tears fell from his eyes as he called out to his dad. Yes, I wanted to bark happily. Yes, Pat has died, but he is here with us in this very moment. The truth is, I feel the presence of all sorts of spirits and things of that nature, and I assume that most of them are family. The one I felt in that room was undeniably Pat's.

Morgan's presence in our lives was a healing that made

the loss of Pat much more bearable to everyone. He was a stout, brown-eyed baby who looked just like Kristina! For months, Casey had been parading around the house saying that he "had a brother in his tummy." Now I could see that he was right, at least about the brother part. The tummy part sort of confused me, but that's kids for you.

My family? Call them crazy, but they made me a proud one-eyed, lumpy-headed pound dog! Now that Morgan was here and Casey had come to know me as his dog, I felt the weight of responsibility growing. Everyone was depending on me now and I couldn't let them down. I cleaned the floor every mealtime, barked when necessary to alert them to visitors, and settled into a role that I was coming to relish.

If Casey's arrival had pulled me closer to home than ever, Morgan sealed the deal. I was here to stay, and life was beginning to take on a whole new meaning for me as guardian and protector of my family. I could now see that it was my nature to change myself in order to best serve those I loved. Though at this point I knew that my nature was a combination of many things, I still imagined that at some point in my life, an answer of answers to the question of my ultimate nature would be revealed to me. At least I knew that I was on the path.

uncle chuck

Now that Pat was gone, Tim was in charge of his youngest brother, Chuck, who'd spent almost his entire life in an institution. It was a huge cluster of buildings in a town near Mt. Rainier called Buckley. Tim had to meet with lawyers, go to court hearings, and fill out lots of other paperwork before he became Chuck's official guardian.

Chuck had been put in the institution by his parents many years before I was born because he loved to twist knobs and almost burned their house down after turning on their gas stove. He was a very short, strong man with a thick neck, oddly chopped hair, and a strange yet wondrous smile. When we visited him, he would jingle a set of keys and make funny noises. I could feel his joy as his voice would rise, and even though nobody else knew what he was saying, I did. He was telling everyone how much he appreciated their love and kindness.

I did learn that being in an institution isn't enough to guarantee you'll be taken care of, even though besides getting snipped, I really can't complain about my institutionalized time at the Humane Society. We went down to visit him every couple of months or so, and as far as I could tell, he was being well cared for.

After a couple of years, Chuck developed cancer and died quickly, leaving one last elder alive on Pat's side. This brother was also a Catholic priest (one of three in that family) that we all knew as Uncle Bill. Uncle Bill came up and said Chuck's funeral mass, and afterwards Casey played "Oh Come Little Children" on his tiny violin as they lowered Chuck into the ground.

Another life and another death, I thought as we left the cemetery to drive back to our busy lives. I'd never really thought about the passing of time, but now I was beginning to consider the notion that I wouldn't be around forever. The thought made me sadder for my family than for myself. I wondered if Chuck and Pat had felt that way too.

the great outdoors

After passing through his spiritual crisis alive, Tolstoy cited several conditions for happiness that I have come to love and embrace. Among these, his first condition for happiness is a life under the open sky in communion with all living things. Wow. When I hear these words, I feel as if they were written for me. This explains why, in general, I do not like staying inside even when hail the size of golf balls is flying all around me.

I also love to camp. To tell you the truth, I love to be outside in any capacity. Give me a 40-degree day with sideways wind and rain and I'll be out in the middle of it, enjoying every second. I've never understood inside dogs. I don't mind being indoors at night when there's food being dropped on the floor, but other than that I'd rather be outside.

We've gone hiking and camping quite a bit. I've climbed mountains, chased deer, barked at bears, and marked hundreds of miles of National Forest trails. My range out there is expansive, and even when I'm in the yard at home, I think of how far my terrain stretches beyond Bellingham. I often imagine myself on those windswept and barren ridges stretching along the Canadian border and only wish there was time to mark the entire Cascade Range stretching into Mexico as my territory. Though I've heard that bears are at the top of the food chain, I don't believe it; I, Ivan the Good, am at the top, and when we're out there, I let everybody know even though the only two things I've ever killed were a shrew and a mole and those were accidental.

I haven't yet told you about my Kristina's parents but her dad is named Tim too, and her mother, La Drene. La Drene is not much of a camper, but she tolerates me, and no doubt is there for me when I'm hungry, with lots of extra scraps and drippings, especially at Thanksgiving. Whenever I'm at their house though, she puts me outside, even when I'm not shedding! This is ironic because she's spent much of her life helping people with disabilities get and keep their jobs. Maybe she thinks one-eyed dogs don't count, but I'd prefer to think that she puts me outside because she thinks I have an important job out there.

Tim Sr. (Kristina's father) is a tall fellow who shares my love for lying in an alpine meadow listening to the wind. He, like me, is a mixed breed who loves to read voraciously. He's a storyteller like Pat, and loves people and pound dogs alike. A man after my own heart! Tim Sr. also loves to row and sail.

Like me, he has spent much of his life in sideways wind and rain though his time on the water was much more daring and exciting than my times in the yard. When he's not on a boat, he's planning hikes with family and friends, always including me. Tim, Sr. calls me a "great mountain dog" and brags to everyone that I'm the greatest dog in the world. He loves to see me with my red pack on, as it was once purchased long ago for Sid my elder, who was two thirds of my weight once I'd grown. In spite of the fact that the straps always feel like they're going to burst from my rippling muscles, I kept our family tradition alive, wearing it proudly for him.

Kevin, Kristina's brother, thinks I'm pretty great too, though he hasn't gone so far as to call me the greatest of all time. He's more of a cat guy, and has a Devon rex feline named Elvis who looks more like E.T. than any cat I've ever seen. That cat goes everywhere with him, and though I've never said this, I believe that Elvis controls his mind. That cat really freaks me out and I find myself avoiding eye contact whenever we're in the same room. Kevin loves the wilderness too, and we often talk of going camping, which brings me back to my original point—camping.

No matter who I'm with, when I'm camping, I'm forever vigilant regarding wilderness hazards. At night, once the campfire has burned down to faint coals, my ears are working overtime to detect the sounds of approaching danger, but unlike most dogs, I almost never bark unless a large mammal like a bear is within range of camp.

When I'm outside, I'm one with my inner wolf, a thousand years old, trotting through places that have called to me in my deepest of dreams. The wilderness gets me more in touch with God, and I would do just about anything to preserve it. The wild is a gift—a place for prophets and pound dogs to find sanity and inner peace.

goat mountain

I've climbed lots of mountains, but there is one that really stands out. Goat Mountain. Maybe someday they'll name a mountain after me. Mt. Ivan? That doesn't sound too impressive. Mt. One Eye? Nah. Three-Legged Peak? Uh-uh. The Snaggletooth? Now we're talking! The Snaggletooth! Yeah, I like that! I can just hear people bragging about bagging the Snaggletooth! I'm sure the name will only come long after I've faded into legend and lore, but it's a nice thought to have a peak named after one of my teeth. I'm not sure why Goat Mountain is named Goat Mountain since I've yet to see a goat up there. Maybe the mountain looks like a goat.

We had just moved from the cabin to our new place and it was Tim's late-spring birthday so he decided to take me for a hike. He filled his little backpack with lunch and we hopped in our little yellow car and sped off toward the mountains. The quick departure didn't seem like any big deal at the time, but later I would realize that it was a big mistake.

It was a cloudy day as I remember, and as we set out, it was starting to rain, which is no big deal for me of course, since I love rain! We climbed up a trail through the forest it seemed for hours, until finally we burst into a large meadow. Above us loomed a high ridge with some rocky outcroppings at the top.

The rain had slackened a bit as we continued on up, while the wind picked up a little. All around us were pinnacles of rock jabbing at the sky shredding the clouds like strands of cotton. The air was pure and cold. I was so strong that I felt that I could climb forever and I was proud to be on such an important mission with one of my family members. We continued up the heather slope leading to a long steep snowfield. Once on this, the going actually got a little easier. Unfortunately, the higher we got the foggier it was getting and the rain was falling again. I dutifully followed Tim as we continued on our way.

It seemed like hours had passed when we finally reached the top of the ridge. Not far away was a rocky summit that we could barely see and now it was raining hard, smacking our faces and my teeth that are exposed by my underbite, as we trudged forward toward our goal. Dogs have long noted that climbing mountains is strictly a human thing. Most dogs would never consider doing something so silly. However, I can't deny that it is highly enjoyable once you're up there, and I do like the view from high places.

After a few minutes, we were standing on a rocky crag

with nothing but the sounds of wind and splattering rain in our ears. Even for me, it was cold. For my master—he apparently hadn't prepared himself well; he was soaked and shivering. I was glad when he told us we were leaving.

Down, down, down we went. After a while, he began skiing on his boots through the snow while I tore after him, nipping him friskily on his gloves. Eventually I saw trees racing by, and knew we had come down a long way. Suddenly he stopped and looked around. I heard him say a word I'd not heard often in a tone of voice that caused me some concern. He looked around as if he had no idea where he was and in a few moments, I realized that it was true. We had descended the wrong way and were lost.

We stumbled down a little farther, though nothing at all looked familiar—a waterfall roared below us and we were nearing some cliffs where the earth seemed to fall away below us. Tim stopped and we both stood silently, listening to the splattering of water on wet rocks far below, and the thudding of our hearts. I could sense danger all around us and knew that we must go back up exactly the way we came, following our footprints. I started upwards in hopes that he would follow and luckily he did.

Up we went, one brutal step after another. I can't deny that I glowed with a warm pride, knowing that Tim was depending on me. I felt like I was doing what I was born to do.

The light was fading from the sky as we plowed upwards through the soggy snow. A couple of hours later and we drew near the top. Now Tim was sweating, and all fear of hypothermia had, for the moment, vanished. As long as we kept moving, we'd be okay. Soon we reentered the heavy fog. All we could see were our slide marks in the snow and even our smell in them was growing faint thanks to the rain and wind.

It leveled out as we stood atop the lonesome barren ridge once more, the wind screaming in our ears. Tim was drenched and shivering again, and we had no idea which way to go when suddenly, as if from an act of God, the clouds lifted and we were soaked in a most brilliant early evening light. We could see all around us. The way home was clear, and we realized immediately our mistake. In the mist and confusion, we had descended the wrong side of the mountain, which would have been disastrous if we had kept going. I joyfully noted that I had played a big part in leading us to safety, and would later appreciate the rough and thankful petting I got as a reward. As it was now, we could see our way clearly back down into the area where we'd left the trees, and with a gleeful yelp, I began prancing and jumping down the steep slope toward safety, freedom, and a ride home. It felt good to give back!

It was almost dark when we arrived back at the car and later on I would hear Kristina lecturing Tim about not being prepared for inclement weather. I was fed a good meal and shown the affection befitting of a hero. I also learned that Kristina was just as worried about me as she was about Tim. I was glad to be home and never wanted to return to those barren slopes again.

family happiness

I haven't yet told you about several other people on Kristina's side who were very important to me. I was glad I got to see them all together at Casey's third birthday party—Kristina's grandmother Janet, her uncle Harry, and her aunt May, along with Kerm, Tim, Sr., Kevin, Colleen, and Auntie Barbara. They all came up to celebrate on a sunny, warm afternoon in June that I'll never forget—it was one of those lazy days where nobody is in a hurry to do much of anything except feast and then feast some more.

We all gathered outside on the lawn and there was much laughter, merriment, and food spilled on the ground—in fact so much that it's almost hard for me to admit that, for the first time in my life, I got a taste of what it's like to be full. Mind you, I wasn't completely full, but at least my stomach was half full, enough to dull the stabbing pains of starvation, tormenting me my entire life. It was also enough to savor for a moment what it must have been like for the Russian aristocracy at every mealtime.

It seemed like everywhere I turned there were pieces of turkey, gobs of mashed potatoes, chunks of cake, and all kinds of other tidbits falling on the ground, fair game for me to wolf down, which of course I did, but it never escaped me that there were other things being relished here at this birthday besides all of the great food—this was a moment with some elders who clearly weren't going to be with us much longer, and in spite of my attachment to the scraps, I was also attached to the warm conversations and laughter floating through the air. Janet, Kristina's grandmother, was practically carried from the van to a seat at the picnic table. She was very old and unable to walk on her own, but none of that mattered; I was warmed by how kind everyone was to her. She giggled at all the attention given to her by Kevin, Colleen, and Kristina.

Uncle Harry and his darling wife, May, were surrounded by their kinsfolk, and were reaping a harvest of the love they'd planted decades before, and later I heard Colleen, Kevin, and Kristina whispering wonderful memories of summers spent with them and how nice it was that everyone was able to get together for what might be the last time. I grew sad at this information, as I was now seeing how quickly things passed in this existence and realized that I must prepare myself and them for more passings, even though I was barely over Pat's. This was the part of life I was admittedly coming to dread, though there's really nothing that can be done about it.

Then there was Kerm, Kristina's grandfather, sitting cherublike in the midst of it all, soaking it in. He wore two hearing aids and sat in his chair, smiling at everyone around him. He would also secretly stuff my mouth when nobody was looking. With him was Auntie Barbara, a proud member of the Red Hat Club, which I think is funny even though I really don't understand it. But Kerm . . . Kerm was really an elder after my own heart.

I must tell you a couple of things that I found to be very funny about Kerm. One was the fact that he wore hearing aids that everyone around him assumed that he needed. I'd hear family members and friends asking him questions about how he was feeling, or if he wanted ice cream with his pie, or if he had taken his meds. Usually questions about pie and ice cream brought a quick answer whereas other questions not so much. I knew that he could hear more than he let on, as evidenced by the conversations Kristina would have with him on the phone. Kerm and I talked too, and I'll tell you, he had no problem understanding me.

I finally realized that Kerm had selective hearing. What a handy thing to have! I could see how that could be used to one's advantage so I began trying it myself, finding that it worked quite nicely when Boris was bugging me, or when it was my bath time, or time to go to the vet.

Evening shadows had begun to fall, when a rousing happy birthday was sung to Casey, and shortly after, everyone loaded up in their cars to head home, relishing the warmth of another successful family get-together. I'll admit that at that point I was ready for a fifteen-hour nap, and felt a bit queasy from all of the birthday cake. Had I known that this would be the last big family gathering on Kristina's side, I might have put off my nap and been more intentional in saying good-bye to everybody. But, I guess I didn't want to believe that in a matter of just a couple of years, Kerm, Aunt May, Janet, and Uncle Harry would be all gone too.

carpé diem

Imagine for a minute having a nose so sensitive that you don't even need eyes to see the world around you. This is close to what a dog's nose is like. And among dogs, I have a particularly effective nose. I've already told you how good my sense of smell is, but it's actually even better than I described earlier; I can smell a male husky on a bush from twenty years ago. I can smell a bear from three miles away, a cougar from ten, and coyotes everywhere. Who needs eyes with a nose like mine? One eye is more than enough, thank you, and in spite of banging the blind side of my head every so often on protruding objects, I do not consider myself disabled.

The canine world is a smorgasbord full of smells old and new. Any dog worth his biscuits will tell you that there are not enough hours in the day, or days in a life, to appropriately sniff everything. When we used to go to the dog park, I would positively lose my mind trying to decipher the layers of odors glued to the grasses and bushes while mental pictures of each dog's face slowly materialized in my brain. Once I swear I conjured up a giant mastodon!

You may wonder why dogs roll in stuff they smell. I'll tell you straight up that I wonder why too. I know I'm the odd-ball, but I've watched too many dogs intently sniffing something disgusting before falling into it in a shivering mass of bliss. I'm proud to say that I'm not like that. While I appreciate these smells as much as any dog, I don't want to take them with me wherever I go. However, there is never enough time to smell it all, so sniff each bush and shrub as if it's your last.

more family happiness

My family and their friends always boast that I am the greatest and most unusual dog in the history of the world. I'm sure there are other dogs more unusual and nicer than me, but I'll take the praise any day.

Throughout the years of my midlife, I could feel myself slowing a little. While I'd always boasted of explosive quickness and believed I could take down a bull elk running at full speed, I also knew I was slowing with each passing year.

I was so proud of my expanding pack, and felt a deeper awareness of life's mystery glowing from within. I could feel the love dripping from the trees, floating pungently about on unseen breezes, rushing in the creeks near our house. I could feel God in just about everything.

I'm one of those dogs who tolerated being petted and

stroked as a pup, and gradually came to relish the gentle touch of my loved ones' hands more than anything else on Earth. I could just lie for hours feeling their hands and hearing those gentle whispers. I could stare at them forever.

I was also even more prone to trot away from an alpha canine without anyone yelling at me. Obviously this wasn't the result of being punished or receiving negative reinforcement. It was simply that anything that I did to disappoint my family caused me sadness. It seemed to be my nature to want to please those who loved me.

I've probably heard the phrase, "Ivan, you are such a good boy," about a million times. I also hear them say I'd better stick around for a long time. When I hear this, I'm afraid that one day they'll think I let them down. I know how much everyone is depending on me.

crime and punishment

I've said this before and I'll say it again—I'll never under-stand why my family cared for me so much, but I know their love is the envy of my brothers and sisters who live out their short lives in cages. Looking back now, I realize I could have done many things differently to save them a lot of grief and money.

One might say that the car accident involving the denting of the Volvo was a fluke, and that the lame eye was destined to be removed anyway, but at least three of the surgeries I've had to endure I'm afraid could have been prevented if I had altered certain behaviors.

One night in late July when I was about to turn nine, I was left outside all night. No big deal—this has happened on occasion before, but on this particular night, I was awakened by the sound of a large ungulate crunching something in his mouth. I'd known about this deer for some time—he was a large buck with an impressive rack and a not so impressive habit of stealing my apples off of my tree in my front yard.

I must admit that resentment had been boiling in me for some time over this thievery, and I'd just about had it. During the summer months I'd been augmenting my meager rations of dog food with these early apples and this greatly helped me maintain my health. Now, with this big buck raiding my yard and eating the forbidden fruit from my tree, I'd gotten "fed" up.

I'd chased him off many times, but he'd always come back and I'd hear the children's voices sing, "look at beautiful Buckskin." Indirectly they were telling me I'd better not chase him and in their presence I wouldn't, though I must admit not tearing after him was extremely difficult.

That fateful night I lay awake listening to the big beast breathing heavily in the darkness, and I could smell the apples on the wretched thief's breath. He probably had no idea that Ivan the Good turned Terrible was lying out untied on this night. I arose from my bed and crept out into the yard.

There we were. Just him and me. His steamy breath swirled around him like smoke in the moonlight, the hot sweetness of my fruit filling the air. I crept forward through the yard one step at a time. Every so often the crunching would cease and I knew he was looking around trying to discern a threat. Each time he began chewing again, I crept closer until I was but twenty feet or so away. I felt the power of all my ancestors coursing through my rigid body, burning with an ancient pride some dogs only dream of. I was going to take down this animal and slay it in my yard. Wouldn't everyone be proud of me? Wouldn't they be forever telling stories about Ivan the Good, the protector of family and ripe fruit?

They would indeed. I crouched, readying for my attack. The time had come to teach this wretch a lesson, one that would send a message to all ungulates to fear Ivan and never dare trespass again.

I lunged in for the kill, snarling my most vicious snarl as the beast lurched about. Suddenly it was all hooves flying about my head as the ground thundered beneath us. The world slumbered as we battled, the stinky beast leaping in panic as my snapping jaws searched for some soft haunch upon which to sink my fearsome teeth. It was Ivan the Good versus Ungulate the Evil, and I'd always believed that Good overcame Evil. Then, it happened.

Actually I'm not sure what happened except that I felt an electric snapping somewhere near my rear right leg as I went flying sideways. The scum kicked me! Down I went, shrieking, only to rise up again, fearlessly snapping, determined to protect all that I held sacred.

Now the beast was rumbling away toward the swamp behind our house as I started to give chase before buckling in a heap. My leg! I couldn't use it! I hobbled after him on three legs until I was sucked into the muck and water was tickling the underside of my belly. I could still hear him thrashing through the mire, and I gave pause, sides heaving, as I celebrated my victory. I showed him!

Run away, coward, back to your dripping mossy woods

and never come to this moonlit meadow again. Now you will think about Ivan the Terrible before you dare try to fill your belly with my apples again!

After some time, and with extraordinary effort, I pulled my front paws from the sucking muck and turned toward home. Victory was not without its cost. My right rear leg burned in agony and I could not put any weight on it. I gimped slowly through the woods, feeling my leg swinging freely beneath my body. Funny, it's never done that before, I thought. Perhaps I can just sleep it off.

The next morning found my family fussing over me with great concern. Ivan, look at you. What happened? I arose and now could hardly feel the leg as I limped into the house. I wished I could tell them of my epic battle and how I saved everyone along with our precious and finite food supply. I couldn't, however, and just wagged my tail weakly. In spite of the pain, I burned with pride over my victory. Yes, it had not been without sacrifice, but would I do it again? Of course I would since it was my nature to risk all to protect those I loved.

what is to be done?

My next major surgery occurred a few weeks after the battle. I learned from Colleen that it was my knee that was blown out, shredded by the dark beast. I love Colleen like I love everyone in my pack, but I was getting more and more scared and confused every time I had to go see her at the Northshore vet clinic. First it was my leg and head with the Volvo. Then it was my eye. Now it was my knee they were going to somehow rebuild.

I knew this trip was probably for the best, though I wasn't too excited about it. I found myself shaking uncontrollably before they put me under and installed a steel plate on my knee to hold it together. After I came to, the first thing I noticed was that my butt felt good yet extremely cold. I didn't realize until later that my entire back end around my knee and haunches were shaved! Why couldn't they have done this before? I wished I was shaved all over! What I didn't like was living inside a small, portable plastic kennel for a week to keep me from ruining my knee again.

I think for the first time in my life, I was keenly aware that I was aging and was not the same dog as I had been, even a year before. Under the natural circumstances of life in the wild, I'd simply have to learn to get along with three legs and do the best I could. This would clearly put my prospects for long-term survival in jeopardy. Under the natural circumstances of life in a family, however, I learned that I must trust and accept my family's care as they could see things in my future that I couldn't see, especially with just one eye.

Over the months that followed, my knee grew stronger and stronger until it was as good as ever. I was grateful, though embarrassed, that they were taking such good care of me, but I kept learning again and again that there is no limit to what loved ones will do for you!

war and peace

Though I have learned about many of the world's great wars and dictatorships, it is still almost impossible for me to imagine people hurting each other. I've never witnessed anything worse than an argument, but even those sorts of things can tear a dog's heart up. I always cower when voices get raised and somehow feel I'm to blame though they never point fingers at me. In fact, besides when I've gotten into the garbage once or twice, I've hardly been scolded. When I hear the stories they tell about people being hurtful, I'm usually sucking food off the floor beneath the table and I fairly shiver.

Apparently people are known to hurt and sometimes kill each other. How is this possible? As a dog I understand that if another male canine violates my territory, there's going to be trouble. Perhaps this is a fair analogy to the current situation plaguing the human race. It certainly has given me much to think about.

I've often entertained the thought of running for public office but Tolstoy believed that a person's political life is destined to corrupt his inner one. I would assume that this is true of a dog's life as well. Just look at any dog show as evidence that vanity governs most of what we do and how we act, derailing us from our own true purpose. However, I have occasionally imagined my true purpose as one who would forever put an end to war and the cruelty of men and dogs. I know in my heart that it begins with love for everyone. Believe it or not, I've even had moments where I've considered running for president. I believe that while I might struggle in the debates, my face would create instant name recognition, and if people were to know my real position on things, I just might get elected.

ivan's political platform

Crime

Upon being elected, I would immediately feed all incarcerated animals (except emotionally unstable and therefore dangerous dogs) the best meal of their lives and then release them back into society. All of their past crimes would be forgiven, and they would be given whatever aid they needed to get on with their lives. I've heard about prisons that hold people and those people would need to be released too (same rules as for dogs) after being fed good meals!

Global Politics

We would immediately withdraw all troops from all countries thus ending our involvement in all wars. Then, I would invite the entire world to sit down and have a big meal together and afterwards take a long siesta on the grass. Call me idealistic, but people don't think clearly when they're hungry or don't get enough sleep; I know I don't. I've heard that, like dogs, many people go hungry, and I just can't stand the thought of that.

I know—you're thinking, "That Ivan, he's an isolationist. Cutting troops makes no sense considering the global inter-connectedness of the modern world." My response is, in order to help the world, we need to help ourselves. We don't spend nearly enough on good things like food for everyone. Apparently we have lots of people and dogs hungry and homeless in America. If I were president, the only war I would declare would be on hunger and homelessness, and my war would also involve the destruction of all weapons that may be used to hurt innocent animals.

Domestic Policies

I would propose fifty billion dollars spent on new off-leash dog parks! I would end leash restrictions in all cities for both canines and humans. I would instigate universal health care for all mammals. I would also propose expanding wilderness boundaries to make them off-limits to logging and mining, but I would allow dogs in national parks.

The Environment

Global warming may be the biggest threat to our future, and from what I've heard, humans' dependence on finite fossil fuel–based resources seems to be a big culprit. Assuming that, I would enact a law requiring people to walk everywhere with their dogs and outlaw cars forever. Think about how dangerous cars are. They kill innocent animals like dogs that are crossing the roads. They also confuse many dogs that are stupid enough to think they are large game animals. Plus they stink. If there were no cars, accidents would no longer occur, pollution would decrease, the world would slow down, people would be less stressed, traffic jams would no longer exist, and animals like me would get to go on more walks. Everybody wins.

The Economy

The first thing I would do as president is abolish all money and corporations and go back to the barter system. Some have suggested that policies like these could throw the economy into a tailspin, but I believe that in the spirit of love and the common good, we would do just fine bartering goods for services. I'd have loved to help people who are less fortunate than myself as a seeing eye dog. Come to think of it, I guess that is what I already am.

Education

As a canine, I'm a big fan of outdoor education and home-schooling. Like I said before, I don't respond well to stimulus-response or coercive behavioral modification techniques. I'm more of a paws-on kind of dog, and I believe experience is our best teacher, even though it's almost killed me a couple of times.

The ultimate solution to the crisis in education is obvious to me, but you first have to look squarely at the problem in order to understand it. Classrooms modeled to sort dogs with two eyes and non-lumpy heads from those with single eyes, lumpy heads, and underbites as a means of promoting a planned global economy in which every dog knows his place aren't fair. As president, I would encourage all mammals to learn at home or outside in the field. It's our only hope left for free thought and freedom in the world.

I know that in today's image-driven society I might be lacking in the good looks necessary for winning, but nobody could ever say Ivan was lacking in face recognition or that Ivan didn't have a dream. I dream big.

My name is Ivan and I approve this message.

carpé diem revisited

Remember I suggested that we should all sniff each shrub as if it's our last? Some people carry on as if they'll live forever. People always say that we dogs lead short lives, but let me tell you, I've already outlived millions of people. A wise person once said that it's not the amount of years in your life that matter, but the amount of life in your years. So many dogs, and I hear at least a few people, are consumed with such self-importance that they miss many of the beautiful shrubs that are popping up all around them.

As I grew older, I felt a glow growing in me that filled me with unspeakable joy, though the steel plate in my knee often throbbed with pain, especially on cold mornings. This steel plate became my ever-present reminder that I was on a one-way journey in which there was no going back. However, the realization that I had aged considerably even from the prior year made no difference to me. What I was becoming was something much different than what I'd ever expected when I was a pup. I wasn't as prone to fight other male dogs who offended me, and simply basking in the warmth of everyone's presence, friend and stranger alike, seemed to be my sole aim in life. Tolstoy says that the more spiritual we become the less attachment we have to our animal nature and I was learning that this was true for me.

education revisited

Okay, I'll admit it—my views on education are not completely my own, but are based on what I've observed within my family. We all know that America is the land of choice, but my family often says that most people are just waiting to be told what to do. My family chooses their own path. I've watched this long enough that I sometimes take it for granted. They choose to grow much of their own food, give birth at home, educate themselves, take care of their elders, and live their own lives. They talk of one day being completely off the grid and living lives that Thoreau, Emerson, and Tolstoy would be proud of.

When Casey was two, Tim built him a playset out of driftwood, rather than buying one of those premade sets. I'm sure the premade thing would have been much safer, but the tower and slide coming off the one he built was much more pleasing to my eye.

Tim also strung a cable between two trees with a little basket on it, and would launch Casey and Morgan from the top and as they flew down the line shrieking and laughing, they'd hit the spring at the end and rise high into the air before being shot backwards by the pressure of the spring. This would terrify me every time, but I guess they were strapped in.

We'd also take our pups backpacking deep into the mountains, often with no trail, and I'd get very nervous when they crossed cold, gushing rivers, knowing that one slip meant disaster as, unlike puppies, human babies can't swim. As I observed this, I came to understand that this was all part of their education, and what I'd later understand as homeschooling was all about taking risks.

My family also helped Tim's mom move to Bellingham so she could be closer to her family. She chose a retirement home not far from our little house and came over several times a week for meals and religious arguments that I'm sure Tolstoy would have found amusing.

During this stretch of life, Tim did just about everything he had to in order to get by. Kristina, as I said, had been a social worker, but now that we had pups of our own, she quit her job. Tim strung together everything from music gigs to substitute teaching, to painting houses and whatever else it took to keep the bills paid and food on the table. Some days he'd come home covered in sweat and paint, other days he'd look more like a teacher, but always he was beaming at his growing family. There wasn't much money in our house, but there seemed to always be enough. There was also more than enough love, and that, I'd come to see, was the greatest wealth of all.

kill your television

As you may have already inferred, we're not big watchers of television. Tim did get cable hooked up once so he could watch the Sonics in the play-offs, but other than that, our motto has been "Kill your television." We're not snooty about it—there's just so much else to do in the way of outdoor activity as well as making art and music and reading books— lots of books, especially to the pups. Not having television is probably a good thing for the kids, but we still do watch movies, so we're a little hypocritical. I've found that this activity can also be hazardous to canine health. Once when I was a little younger I saw on the screen the image of a most terrifying looking animal with a fearsome face, jagged teeth, and a hideous lower jaw. This beast seemed to be challenging me so I did what every good dog should do—I charged the television set and almost knocked it over as everyone screamed at me.

What? I was just protecting you. Why are you so mad at me? Then they were all laughing. What's so funny? How'd you like it if I laughed at you? Eventually I realized that the animal on the television screen was a home movie starring me. Ouch! Now my motto really is *Kill Your Television!* especially if you see a one-eyed, underbitten pound dog staring at you!

i wasn't much of a singer anyway

This is sort of embarrassing to talk about, given how thoroughly preventable it was, but nonetheless I will. I wish I could adequately apologize for this but I can't. I know this one cost them a pretty penny.

About leashes—I would argue that while leashes are effective ways of controlling a dog's wandering instincts, for most dogs this limiting of territory creates confusion and breeds neurosis. For me, though I've never been neurotic, I have had consistent problems with my short-term memory along with the dubious encouragement of certain squirrels. The results of this are what led to surgery #4.

Like I said earlier, Tolstoy's first condition of happiness is a life spent under the open sky in communion with all living things. Amen, brother! There was only one problem with my life under the open sky, and that was related to the rope that I was sometimes tied to as a result of my wanderings. This is what led to my fourth (but not final) surgery . . .

After the incident with Jessica and in my younger years, I found myself, more often than not, tied to a rope attached to my apple tree, especially when my family left and, for whatever reason, couldn't take me with them. Every time that car pulled away, I was convinced that I was being punished for my past sins. I would sink into a deep melancholy and just lie there under the apple tree as each excruciating minute passed by. Though it was probably not terribly long, it felt like eternity.

Some people have theorized that time passes very quickly for dogs; indeed, that we have little sense of time at all. Trust me when I say that this is a lie! Time moves very slowly when you're tied to a tree with nobody but annoying squirrels chattering at you and telling you what to do.

If my family left me, I could hardly blame them, though I would grow mad with worry that they might need my protection and I wouldn't be able to give it to them. Thoughts like these were almost unbearable. Then, when I'd practically given up all hope, I'd hear the slow crunching of tires on gravel as the car rolled into view.

"Run!" the squirrels would squeak, and at their cue, I would leap to my feet and explode toward my family at full speed, forgetting I was tied to the tree. As soon as I would reach the end of the leash, I'd be snapped sideways, often landing on my ribs gasping and heaving for air. My throat would burn and for several moments I'd be unable to breathe. I'd then hear the squirrels chattering hysterically in the branches above me. This would happen again and again, year after year, as I couldn't figure out the relationship between the rope and my throat.

Here I was, years later, with a prickly throat that felt like it was full of splintered glass. This feeling would sweep over me every hour or so, and I would find myself retching and heaving with difficulty breathing. Colleen called it laryngeal paralysis, but I just called it a sore throat. She said that sometimes dogs that get this die from suffocation when the larynx collapses suddenly like a saxophone reed. There would need to be another operation to prevent this from happening, plus she found some fatty lumps around my chest that needed to be taken off. I was okay with it though I was worried that this was going to cost some more serious money.

After the surgery, I was told not to bark for two weeks, which wasn't easy. My hair was shaved off of my neck which, again, I loved, though I looked very strange. Once I did start barking again, my voice was different—more of a hoarse squeak and not the fearsome roar I was accustomed to using when necessary. I accepted this change as an inevitable condition of life though it was embarrassing to consider how thoroughly preventable it could have been. I learned that we should never run beyond the limits of our leashes, but instead learn how to free ourselves from them. Once we do that, we will run forever.

keep it wild!

One day not long after the throat surgery, my family was sitting around the dinner table with our good friend from the far northern reaches of Alaska, Sarah James. She is a Gwich'in tribal member. The Gwich'in are the last subsistence tribe in North America, surviving on the Porcupine caribou, and Sarah had been appointed by her elders to travel around the U.S. raising awareness about the Gwich'in culture and the threat to their way of life by the oil companies who want to open up the Arctic National Wildlife Refuge to drilling. Pat had already taught me the importance of elders' instructions so I understood the importance of Sarah's mission. The Gwich'in depend on the Porcupine Caribou for their survival and the oil companies want to drill right into the heart of the caribou's calving grounds! I was now learning more things about humanity that I must admit were breaking my heart.

I should note that, over the years, our house has served as a stopover and resting place for people like Sarah who are trying to save the world. I've enjoyed meeting these people, and they seem to enjoy me as well. Now that Sarah was here again, I listened with great interest as she explained what was going on, and in the course of the conversation, another topic came up that made me shudder and would give me nightmares. Not only were the caribou, moose, and other animals that lived in that particular area threatened, there was a sinister action that was taking place all over Alaska, an action that was entirely legal. I couldn't believe it was legal!

I suppose you'd like to know what it is. It's with great difficulty that I tell you, but tell you I will. There is a campaign called the Alaskan wolf kill that allows hunters, with the blessing of law enforcement, to fly around in helicopters or planes gunning down my wolf cousins with automatic weapons. This is apparently done as a means of increasing the big game population, but what is most upsetting to me is the fact that many Alaskans and people from other parts of the country actually think this is a good idea. Do they understand that wolf packs are like families, and when certain members are killed, the rest of the pack mourns and loses its ability to function and even survive? Do these people dare own dogs? If so, how could they ever look their dog in the eye and support something like this?

Perhaps it's the same type of person who would kill coyotes for fun. Now, I don't like coyotes, and you already know how they tried to kill me, but I would never want them harmed by someone simply because they were a threat to me or our chickens, or even Boris! I do believe that Boris supports the wolf kill, but that's a cat for you—a four-legged critter governed almost entirely by self-interest.

For me, this was appalling! Every rational creature knows that there is a delicate balance of life that is meant to be honored and maintained by those with the ability to reason, but most often this is not the case. What's even more appalling is that some of these hunters don't even want the meat from their kills. I cannot imagine all of that good meat going to waste.

Sarah informed us that there were many people including hunters who were fighting to stop this practice, and that made me feel a little better. Still, I found this news to be extremely unsettling, and the saddest thing of all was, as I said before, I was beginning to understand that some people weren't very nice. After Sarah's visit, I have two things to say to the people of Alaska—keep your paws off of my wolf brothers and keep the Arctic National Wildlife Refuge a safe place for caribou!

goat mountain revisited

It was in late February many years later that, to my dismay, we returned to Goat Mountain. This time it was late in the winter of a great drought. There was very little snow in the mountains, and Tim wanted to climb it again with me. We drove out to the trailhead and trudged up the switchbacks for a couple of hours before finally bursting out into that same low basin, which was now covered with snow. However, on the high ridge angling up towards the rocky summit, much of it was barren, the grass brown and dead.

Near the top was that long snowfield, and from where we were, it looked like it would pose little problem for us. We worked our way up towards the summit, and as we grew closer, the way grew much steeper than I'd remembered. I whimpered, not wanting to go any farther, but Tim urged me on. I dutifully obeyed, but in spite of the pure winter sunshine on us, I felt something sinister about the place.

The last stretch involved a terrifyingly steep ascent up a knife-edged snow ridge, but as far as I could tell, the footing was okay. Like a ladder, we climbed until at last we stood atop that same rock crag we'd stood upon on that fateful birthday seven years prior.

Tim let out a holler, and I just sat there waiting patiently for the command to go. The wind fluttered and howled as we stood there. I felt immortalized in the majesty of the moment there with nothing but open sky, frigid air, and the earth falling away from us. Finally, Tim said it was time and we turned to leave.

He thought the best way down was to slide directly into the basin, so we moved sideways across the ridge a little before beginning our descent. Tim started but something froze me in my place. As soon as he began moving, he careened wildly out of control for about fifty feet before finally skidding to a stop. Sensing danger for him, I lunged downwards towards him, intent on saving him when I realized that I was sliding over glazed ice, unable at first to stop.

"Stay there, Ivan!" he yelled and I managed to slide to a stop above him. Below us were cliffs (hadn't we done this before?) and I felt the tingling of danger in my legs. He slowly climbed toward me. "Just stay there, Ivan. Stay there, boy. It's okay." There was something calming in his voice and I felt the warmth of his reassurance. He kept repeating himself as he drew closer. It would be okay as long as I listened to him. I whined and shifted my weight a little. That was all it took, and suddenly I was skidding downhill over the ice again, out of control, unable to stop. I shrieked in terror, trying to dig my claws in as I spun around and around. This was it, I thought, though I wasn't sure exactly what "it" was. As the cliffs below us drew close, I suddenly felt something grab me.

Tim held me by my harness, having perfectly timed his grab before I would have slid by and over the cliff to a fate I don't even want to think about. We stood there in silence yet our hearts were pounding so loud they seemed to echo like drums in the valley. I felt the fear in him as well as my own. Yet again, we had underestimated the dangers of this place and almost paid the price.

Now we had to traverse a couple hundred yards of steep ice blown hard by the relentless winds. Though the last thing I wanted to do was move anywhere, I knew we couldn't stay where we were. One step at a time we progressed back towards our original boot tracks and safety. Each step back brought the danger of sliding again, and a couple of times, I felt my claws giving way on the ice. After a long tense stretch, we finally reached our original tracks and breathed deeply for a long while before resuming our downward descent.

We had made it once again off of Goat Mountain. This time for sure I would never venture back to those lonesome dangerous ridges again, unless of course Tim decided he wanted to. Thank goodness he didn't. I'd now learned that it was my nature to trust the ones I loved when I was most afraid. When I was younger, I probably wouldn't have listened to anybody if I was in such danger. After telling this story upon our return home, Kristina called Tim a bonehead. I'd never heard that one before, but I trust that it was appropriate.

new beginnings

It was this same year that we got some big news. After scraping by for years, Tim finally landed a job teaching high school English in an alternative school! At last there would be some security under our roof. Tim would have a lot more freedom to do what he wanted than most public school teachers, and this was the gravy on the dog food, as we say.

I listened with interest to the stories he brought home every day. He worked with a compassionate staff of big-hearted people who loved helping disadvantaged and often damaged kids get their lives together. Some of the kids almost reminded me of strays as they wandered in and out of his school searching for a permanent and stable place to stay while they got on their feet.

The funniest joke of all was that he was now making

more money than he'd ever made before, which really says a lot about what we were living on prior to the job. In fact, we'd never seen such money flowing though our house on a consistent basis. I noticed a definite increase in dog snacks, which was great! After what Tim had been making before, this was like winning the lottery! Of course, it's all relative, and when you're used to living month to month on little money, a job like teaching is going to make one feel pretty rich. There was a noticeable lack of stress at the end of each month, even though there was still barely enough to pay the bills, which seemed to continually grow in size like the pups.

We moved away from our house to a new one in the country, and suddenly, we were living the dream! I knew I'd miss my apple tree and the swamp but I did like our new place once we were settled.

A few acres of blowing grass, some huge trees towering over us, a thundering river nearby, and mountains popping up everywhere. There was even a big apple tree for me, though I quickly learned that the apples wouldn't ripen and fall until late September and they weren't as sweet and soft as my summer apples on the old tree, and I might have to compete with bears instead of ungulates. Still, what was there for a dog not to love? This would be the site for the ultimate homeschooling experiment, and where I learned most of what I was put on Earth to learn. At least this is how I saw it at the time.

Some say that education is critical to our national survival and that other nations are getting ahead of us. I suppose this means that kids around the world are in a sort of global Iditarod Race, but what I think we really need to also learn how to grow food, nurture pups, play and compose music, produce literature and art, win the love of other pound dogs, and learn to bark nicely at each other. I think schooling needs to nurture these ideas and values since we all know that the Iditarod Race has only one winner and that countless dogs have died or been severely injured in the race for glory.

What I've already observed from this great homeschooling experiment should open a few eyes. First of all, let me say that Kristina is the greatest teacher I've ever known, and I'm not just talking about for the pups, though there are some things I do want to share with you about them.

Take our oldest pup, Casey, for example. He loves stories and both Kristina and Tim read to him even before he was born. His vocabulary was way better than most dogs and people his age, but up until age 9, he was reluctant to read on his own. I even began wondering if this kid should be in regular school. My family just waited it out, and one day Casey found himself absorbed in full-length novels, bird encyclopedias, and all sorts of interesting books. The best thing of all is that he loves reading so much that he can't seem to get enough of it! What was even more impressive is that he has real passion for life; he plays exquisite violin music, draws and studies birds, plays soccer, and ties trout flies. I'm afraid that school might have crippled those passions.

Then there's Morgan . . . my little buddy Morgan. At six years old, he could stand in front of an audience at birthday parties or Tim's gigs, and tell stories to the audience like it was nothing! He loves to act and is learning to love reading and playing violin. This pup's spirit of adventure is inspiring, and he loves to bring people together. He also wants to do everything in his power to save the world, and both he and Casey often use their birthday parties to raise money for important causes.

Many of our friends in town wondered how such a family of oddballs would fare in the country where it was said that people like to keep to themselves. My family is not only bold, they're fearless.

After moving out to the country, Kristina began wandering around the neighborhood introducing us to everybody. And of course, everybody loved her. The first thing that went in was a huge garden and she had a farmer from down the road out there taking directions from her as he tilled it with his tractor. As the earth was turned and the smell of life steamed into the air, there was a new feeling of hope and joy in the entire family. The boys were out climbing trees and chasing each other. Tim was building a shed, and our goddess beamed over all of us as she orchestrated everything. Trees were planted, blackberries cleared, wetlands restored, garbage hauled away, porches built, music played, birthdays celebrated . . . it was busy. In the midst of it all, we'd wander over to the river to swim in the baking summer sun, and life swelled with contentment and meaning.

Soon, the rewards of planting were tasted—fresh vegetables appeared on everyone's plates (even mine!). Now the talk had shifted to how we might go even further off of the grid. I'd known for some time that the grid was set up to create energy dependency on big corporations while preventing individuals from exercising full control over their lives. We came to see every enterprise that way, corporations and institutions set up to put and keep people in their place, and to stop them from reaching their full potential. Not us! Potential was everywhere and I, Ivan the One-Eyed, was basking in unspeakable contentment. Thoreau's dream had been reborn and you could almost feel the sun smiling on us every day, even when it was raining.

I found myself growing more and more content to just watch everyone around me, and this made me understand the contentment of Kerm and Pat in their last years. If I never moved from my bed again but was able to watch them happily growing up, I'd be satisfied. Life was so good, but I could feel strange changes occurring deep within me. My family seemed happy, too, and Boris adjusted well to the new surroundings though he was his usual paranoid self, thinking that the owls and coyotes had conspired to kill him.

elders

It was late in that first summer that Tim and Kristina moved Tim's mother into our house to live out the last of her remaining years. She had declined noticeably in the past couple of years, and now in the new place, there was room to move her in. I was noticing something different—her memory was failing and she wasn't inclined to argue politics and religion as much. Bernice was now using a walker to get around since her eyesight had grown so bad and she was in danger of falling. After she moved in, I found myself thinking of Pat and Sid again, finally understanding that life was coming full circle and that this was the normal, natural way of helping an elder along on her journey. Once, long ago, Bernice had cared lovingly for her pups; now it was time to repay that kindness.

When Pat had died years before, we'd all spent months going through all of the stuff in Tim's childhood house, and in the process, Tim had came across many old photos, paintings, and other memorabilia that painted a picture of a very complex woman.

Bernice was one of the first women to ever attend the Art Institute of Chicago, and the pictures I saw revealed a goddess of great beauty herself. Her skill as a painter was unmatched by other girls her age, and as a result, she was granted admission to this exclusive school.

She grew up in a small house in a Polish neighborhood and was a teenager during the Great Depression. Her father Joseph was a craftsman and woodworker who'd spent most of his life in Russia though he was of Lithuanian descent. Bernice would tell story after story about their dog Schubert and how he would sleep in their beds and climb up on the dining room table to slurp food out of a bowl. Apparently Joseph had no rules whatsoever regarding their household, and Schubert was the great beneficiary of a family who loved their dog as one of them. Lucky guy! I know my family loves me (in spite of their scanty food portions), but it sounded like Schubert was really living the dream!

Bernice also volunteered much of her time with the United World Federalists and was a peace activist before the hippies were even born. Tolstoy would have been proud! Then came her love affair with religion and while she never let go of her early roots, she became a lover of the Catholic tradition. She always told everyone that her life didn't really begin until she had a family, and once she did, she mostly stopped painting, though she did do portraits of her loved ones. I think she wanted to do one of me, but I couldn't stand still long enough for it to work out.

Bernice was deeply dedicated to her family. Now, as she had reached the pinnacle of her twilight years, it was time for her to be taken care of. In spite of the personality differences and challenges between her and Tim, he and Kristina welcomed the opportunity to give back especially since, as Tim noted, she was forgetting about most of the things she once liked to argue about.

We spent that first summer just hanging around, walking over to the river to swim and fish, and building fires outside in the evening time. One thing we didn't do, which was sort of strange to me, was go camping. Maybe we were too busy moving in. If there was only one thing I would change about that magical summer, it would have been a camping trip. It was a good summer, though I did get yelled at for diving into the water after a fish.

That July, a raven showed up and hopped around on the ground for a few hours. I watched it being hand fed by the kids, and thought its behavior very strange. I've heard stories about ravens and owls having mystical powers, and must admit I was very curious. All the doors in the house were closed up, probably to prevent me from going outside, but eventually Morgan came inside and left one open. I just thought I'd go have a closer look at the bird and perhaps give it a sniff, but when I opened the screen door with my nose and wandered outside, it immediately flew up in the air and directly over me, staring at me as if it had seen me before or something. It landed in a tree and the kids were very upset that I'd scared it off. I felt bad, but what's a one-eyed dog to do? It wasn't like the bird was the first thing I'd ever scared off.

I wondered if Adam would be able to find our new house if he did come back to visit. I wasn't sure how good Adam's nose was. If he was like most people, it probably wasn't so good.

Fall time rolled around, and we settled in, cutting wood and finishing projects as we got ready for winter. A pack of coyotes started showing up at night bugging me to chase them, but I never did. I'm not stupid! I also learned that it was my nature to accept and adapt to life changes, even though I'd loved our old place just fine. In fact, I didn't care where we lived as long I was with those I loved.

b.i. (before ivan)

I recently learned that my family had some great dogs in the past. Tim grew up with a beautiful purebred Norwegian elkhound named Tinkerbell who lived until his early teens. According to the stories, she was a great family dog who once tried to eat a bass plug and had to get the hooks surgically removed at the vet. The thought of this just makes me shudder! Tinker also ate a bunch of baby chickens, which caused Tim and his sister some grief. Tinker also hated the water, and suffered during the summer months due to her heavy coat.

After she died, the family got a female German shepherd, and thanks to the feminine influence among the household's human population, she was named Petrushka after Igor Stravinsky's famous ballet. Her nickname was Trishka, and get this—she had an orange tabby they called Nijinksy, named after Vaslav Nijinsky, the Russian ballerina who played the lead role in "Petrushka"! When I told Boris this, he was hysterical at the notion that we weren't the first cat and dog tandem with Russian names!

Trishka sounds like she was truly an amazing dog too—Tim even boasted that she was as smart as I am, and had a nose that actually put mine to shame, which is really hard for me to believe. She was loyal and, like me, a lover of all people. Tim says that she was a stick dog (which would have been a little annoying), but she was also a great mountain dog. Apparently, she hated male dogs and would often attack them unprovoked! I wish I could have known her. She developed severe hip dysplasia when she was six and died before she was ten, leaving her family heartbroken. She sounds like she was the ultimate dog.

Purebreds definitely have something I don't have, and I've probably got some things that they don't. In my pound dog opinion, though, we're all just dogs, big and little, and it's what's in the heart that counts the most.

who i might have become

sometimes wonder who I might have become if I hadn't found a loving home. I fear the things I might not have learned. I fear that, without the love of my family, I might have grown mean like Ivan the Terrible. I might have learned only that life is the never-ending struggle with others for a limited food supply, and that self-gratification is the highest level of individual attainment. I might have learned that it's okay to bite, it's okay to fight, and it's okay to kill regardless of the circumstances. I might have come to understand humans as cold, indifferent beings. I might have learned that living apart from others is the only way to keep a dog's heart safe from being broken. I might have learned that taking risks to help others isn't worth the broken heart you'll have in the end. I might have come to believe that the fulfillment of my animal nature is all there is to life. I might have learned that looks are everything, and that there's no place in the world for the one-eyed and underbitten. I'm just glad that I never learned these things.

pound dogs

I know there are lots of people who are truly saints that support their local humane societies found throughout the country. I've heard stories from other dogs about people adopting pets from their local chapters who are old and dying, just to give that animal the experience of being loved. I know there are many people who simply can't relate to other people but pour their hearts and souls into caring for us, simply because we are, for whatever reason, the next best thing to being human. In my opinion, people who work relentlessly to stop things like the Alaskan wolf kill that I was howling about earlier are some of the country's biggest hidden heroes. I also consider heroes those individuals and rescue organizations that dedicate themselves to finding homes for the poor, unwanted, and underbitten. I count myself lucky to have been brought to the good folks at the Humane Society of Skagit Valley when I was a pup. They understand that unwanted animals, be they purebred or mongrel, crave only one thing and that's companionship.

If you love us, we will love you more. If you save us, you will rarely be sorry. We may not be the purebreds so sought after, or we may be the purebreds who are broken and abandoned, but one thing we all have in common is that we will dedicate ourselves to you, asking nothing in return.

slowing down

It was probably in mid-September that I first noticed the pain in my left leg. Actually, I felt the pain growing for some time, but it became acute in September. I could tell something was wrong with it months before, but I attributed it to growing older. After all, I was no longer a pup. I was still in pretty good shape and confident I could still take down a Grizzly Bear or Bull Moose if necessary, so a little ache in the knee wasn't going to kill me. It was when others started noticing my limp that I became concerned.

Mind you, my concern wasn't related to my own condition, but was in relation to theirs. I didn't want to cost them another penny—they'd already spent far too much on this lumpy-headed canine. My concern was that I'd somehow blown out my knee on something else and that I'd have to go to Colleen to have another surgery. I didn't mind the shaving part, but more surgery? No! I tried my hardest not to limp, but everybody still noticed and also expressed concern over my apparent attempt to hide it.

One morning when I heard someone stirring, I struggled to my feet and shuffled into the kitchen, snuffling and snorting. (I try to make as much noise as I can without barking, which hastens the speed at which I get my morning meal. This has worked my entire life, and I don't mind being gently scolded as a result.) Usually by the time my first scoop hits the bottom of my bowl, saliva has been pouring off of my jaw into a pool on the floor (my choice!) and a towel is fetched. In spite of this, it still probably takes no more than forty-five seconds from the time someone enters the kitchen to the time I'm gulping those scant mouthfuls of precious food.

This morning I was excitedly anticipating breakfast when suddenly my back legs shot out from under me. I hit the floor hard, shrieking as a searing pain flashed through my leg. My family rushed to my aid, helping me off the floor and to my feet. Good job, Ivan, I thought. You really did it this time.

My leg tingled and burned from the accident and I thought my knee was done for good. Not wanting to allow a useless leg to get in the way of a good meal, I gimped over to my food dish and gobbled up my breakfast. This seemed to make everyone feel better and of course it made me feel better too. They helped me outside and as I limped out onto the grass, I was surprised my leg was already feeling a little better.

Over the next week, the leg actually felt much better and I was relieved that I wasn't going to cost anyone any more trouble and money. I was taken for walks along the river and took one great one in the mountains. I'll never forget that walk—the smell of fall was heavy in my nose and the rushing creeks filled my soul with peace. It was so good to be alive.

Things went along like this for another few weeks, until I noticed one day that the pain, along with the limp was back. This time it hurt more than it had before. An appointment was scheduled to meet with Colleen.

Everyone at the clinic seemed glad to see me. I've got to tell you a little about Northshore Veterinary Hospital where Colleen works. They are the most wonderful people in the world and everybody there knows me by name. I must be a celebrity; at least they treat me that way. They even kept my eyeball in a jar as a souvenir. I think it's because I'm sort of Colleen's dog but I think every animal that walks through their doors is treated well. I'm sure they could all tell how scared I was as I was shaking uncontrollably. I knew that they felt badly, and I wished I could control it; it wasn't their fault. It was mine.

Colleen took me up to her office and started moving my knee around just like she had when I blew the other one out. "I don't get it," she whispered. After a while, she took me into another room and told me she was going to take a picture of it. Afterwards, she stared at the picture, and I noticed there were tears in her eyes and my heart tingled with sorrow for her.

I've got to tell you a little more about Colleen. She's really like a second mother to me, and if she were the one who had found me at the Humane Society, I would have been just as well off. She's beautiful like Kristina, and people are always mistaking them for each other. That should tell you a lot right there. She became a veterinarian for all the right reasons, but primarily because she loves animals, especially pound dogs. She has had a couple of pound dogs herself. Even though I really don't like going to the vet, I always know I'm in good hands with Colleen.

Later on that night, everyone gathered around me. People were crying which was a little embarrassing. I felt so bad for them, especially the kids, and knew it had something to do with me. I must have really blown my knee out this time to have upset everybody so much. I wanted to tell them that I was okay and that in spite of the limp I'd get along just fine. The phone seemed to be ringing all evening and there was talking in the other room along with more tears. They told me that many of my old friends were calling me to say hi. Why was everyone so upset? People just need to calm down, I thought.

The next morning when I tried to get up, I almost fainted it hurt so badly. I could no longer put any pressure on the leg without sharp daggers stabbing upward through my hip. This was no good at all. My family tried to help me outside, but I wanted to immediately head for my bed and lie down. If I just laid down maybe everything would be okay and people would stop being so upset.

Over the next few days I learned that I had cancer and I knew it was bad news. Another appointment was scheduled with Colleen, and this time I had a feeling it was going to be a big one. I really wasn't very worried, having learned that even when things get really rocky, someone who loves you will be there to pick you up and carry you. Of course, I'd do the same for them a million times over.

who needs four legs?

When I was brought in for my next appointment, everyone at the clinic said hi to me and scratched my head. It was good to see them, but I was shaking a bit. Colleen brought me upstairs to a room with a metal table. When she brought out the big syringe, I gulped a bit. Okay, I thought, let's just get this over with. She hovered over me for a moment and I knew this was going to be different from the other surgeries. Suddenly she smiled and rubbed my ears which made me feel better immediately. Then she stuck me and that was all I remembered.

For days it seemed as if I was having the strangest dreams. First I'd be running with a huge pack of one-eyed wolves, and then I'd see my family standing over me smiling, their breaths steaming in the cold air. I felt a keen sense of elation like I was being set free, but then I'd become aware of something tugging and tearing at my leg. This went on forever it seemed. Eventually, I awakened and all was calm. Colleen was whispering to me and the first thing I saw was her smile.

She took me outside, and the funniest thing of all was that, while the pain was gone, I could no longer feel my leg. It was gone too! Weird! Every step I took, I felt myself buckling to the ground. What was this all about? I could handle the eye being taken out because it was useless. I understood the rebuilding of the knee as necessary. I certainly supported the surgery on my throat, as I feared choking to death, but this? My leg? How would I run with only three? How would I protect the family?

Colleen was begging me to use my good back leg, so I did. It wasn't easy and even after a few tries I could go only a few feet before my good leg burned unbearably under the crushing weight of my body. Man, this was tough!

I didn't ever begrudge Colleen for taking off my leg, as I knew she must have needed to, but at first I wasn't happy being a three-legged dog. I stayed in the kennel another night, and the next day my family came and got me. I was so excited to see them and get out of there before they decided to take my head off or something! I found myself lunging to greet Tim. Colleen was very happy about this, and said I was doing much better. She must have had a lot of faith in me, because she insisted that I'd be able to adapt to three legs just fine, once I got used to it. She said I had a great spirit and that made me feel so good.

Upon my return home, I was showered with attention and given more affection than I can even describe. There were a lot of tears from the kids as well, but I tried to lick them away the best I could. I wouldn't trade this feeling of being loved for anything else in the world. The next few weeks would be spent learning how to walk again and getting ready for Christmas.

Already I was over the loss of the leg. It didn't matter. All that mattered was being with those who loved me. The thought that many dogs and people will never know what it's like to be needed in the way that I am made me sad. I wish others could know how good a dog's life could feel.

taking care of business

Bernice was failing too. I could feel it in her. She is a lover of books, but her reading and hearing abilities were so reduced that she was soon forgetting everything that was happening around her. Her reading was aided by a single lighted magnifier that she used to scour her big-print books, and her hearing was aided by a headset that, even after countless times practicing, she could barely figure out how to use, even though there was only an on/off switch and a volume knob to worry about. Still, she never pitied herself but instead accepted the changes of aging as inevitable.

Only two years before, she had finished a beautiful painting of Morgan, and in spite of her poor sight, I was impressed by the likeness she'd achieved. Now, she patrolled the house with her walker, bumping into things and knocking them over. Nobody complained much as they seemed to be more impressed with how well she was doing. I just tried my best to stay out of her way so she wouldn't fall on me or my good leg.

The boys were also very helpful to her, often reading and playing violin to her to pass the time, and that's when I realized what a vital part of their education this was—learning how to cope with both a failing elder and a failing dog. What more important lessons can be gleaned from life than that? One benefit of Bernice's condition was that it took some of the attention off me, and I was grateful for this, as I'd been receiving far too much lately. Another benefit was that she dropped a lot of food on the floor.

Kristina was now helping Bernice into the bathtub, and again, I thought of old Sid in that wheelbarrow. I remember how funny I thought that was when I was a pup. I wasn't laughing now, but was more awestruck by the selfless nature of my beautiful Kristina, staying positive and accepting things as they were, save for the occasional moments of exasperation and tears.

What an education, learning both how to live and how to die! This thought hadn't occurred to me until this point, but once it did, I could not shake it. I only hoped I'd outlive Bernice, so as to help her on her way the best I could while providing comfort to those I loved.

adapting

I'll tell you straight out that my family would never pro-
long life any longer than it was supposed to be prolonged,
but if they had done nothing, I wouldn't have made it past
Christmas and thus would never have been able to give you
my pound dog perspectives. With three legs, and an undy-
ing sense of optimism, I plowed forth into the holiday season
with renewed vigor. Bernice even seemed more chipper, and
I'd like to think that it was my attitude that helped lift her
spirits.

We christened our new house with its first tree, and the
children were busy making and wrapping presents, baking
cookies, and taking me for walks while Tim and Kristina
took me for runs. That's right; you heard me. I could run! In
fact, it was easier to run than to walk. Who needs four legs?

I thought, joyously. We'd do laps around our field, and once I was moving, I was unstoppable, and given the fact that I was never quite a greyhound in the first place, I was doing as well as I ever had. Life was good, and I was getting strong again. Maybe we'd hold off on this death thing for a while after all.

I certainly couldn't deny that while I missed my other leg, I sure didn't miss the pain. I must admit, though, that it took some practice getting used to performing the day-to-day canine routines and functions. While I knew I wouldn't be climbing any more mountains, I still planned on getting around the neighborhood on a regular basis as my boundaries for marking still ranged far and wide.

surrounded by love

I was finally getting it—that is, this meaning of life. Maybe my lumpy head was stepped on a little too hard when I was a pup, but now I understood that everything we'd done to help Sid, Pat, and Bernice along had somehow prepared me for these times.

Kristina was now heavy with another pup, and as if teaching two boys weren't enough, Bernice's hearing and sight was all but gone and Kristina was now helping her find her way around the house. It was hard for Bernice to accept the help, but I guess there comes a time when it takes a certain amount of grace to receive help with thanks, and not be embarrassed by it.

I was, at this point in life, convinced that no one could see Kristina the way that I could. Like most male dogs and people, Tim was so busy trying to mark his turf with his music, writing, and teaching that he missed some of the little things that I could clearly see that made Kristina extraordinary.

I wanted the world to see that my Cosmic Goddess of Love was truly worthy of the title. If there was another human being who suffered, be it through war or natural disasters, or a rainforest or animal going extinct, Kristina wanted to help. She didn't want to argue politics but to live her beliefs. She understood that we are born to love whether we know it or not, and the level of our happiness is found in our service to others.

She didn't always get along with Bernice, but she continued her work with selfless abandon. She also nurtured our pups including the one she was carrying, and worked the cold winter earth in anticipation of the spring plantings. Ah, spring. What I wouldn't give to see another spring with my goddess and her lovely family.

the good . . .

Thoreau once said that we should not "be simply good, but be good for something." Ivan the Good has tried to heed this advice. I'm not sure that I've been good for much more than ten grand in vet bills, but apparently my family thinks I'm worth something. What I've learned is that dogs who bark about how smart or great they are usually aren't, and intelligence is highly overrated anyway. If you look at all the problems in the world, they're mostly created by the ones who think they're so smart. And what would you rather be, good or smart? Being smart doesn't mean you'll be happy, but being good at least gives you a chance. Clearly, as I look back over my life, I can't say that I've been the smartest dog, but despite my looks I've tried to live up to my name Ivan the Good.

Oscar Wilde wrote a novel called *The Picture of Dorian*

Gray, in which his strange protagonist is so consumed with his own appearance, immortalized in a painting, that he never develops compassion for the well-being of others and ends up only living for his own egotistical fulfillment. The more he lives for himself, the more miserable he becomes, and the more hideous his face becomes in the painting. I've seen a few dogs live only for themselves, so I can understand the meaning behind this story. I'm just glad that nobody tried to immortalize me in a painting. I mean, how much worse can my face get?

sticking around

My beautiful Colleen informed us that although I had cancer, I was otherwise an extremely healthy dog for my age. She suggested that chemotherapy might lengthen my life by up to a couple of years though eventually the cancer would come back and kill me. I wish I could have told everyone not to bother, but I doubt they would have listened anyway. I had a feeling that no matter what was done, I was destined to be leaving this world sooner rather than later and it would be best just to accept that, though there was still an unanswered question regarding my nature that I hoped would be resolved before I departed.

I found myself worried about my family and what they would do without me to guard and protect them. At first, the thought of them getting another dog was too much for old

Ivan to bear. I knew I was one-in-a-million and you don't go out and find a one-eyed, three-legged, underbitten dog with a lumpy head just anywhere. On the other hand, I knew the Humane Society was full of dogs, unique in their own ways, who were nurtured by some of the most compassionate people you'll find anywhere. In fact, the more I thought about it, the more I wanted to tell them not to wait until long after I was gone—that there would be another, and they'd know him right away.

Sure enough, in my dreams, I started seeing a familiar looking dog with skunk-like markings on his face, though his jaw was normal and he had two eyes. He was a little annoying in that he loved to lick my protruding teeth but he was a far cry from the alpha that I am, and thus we got along playing together. He came to me with such frequency that I began to think there might be something to this.

After Christmas, things progressed more or less without incident for the next couple of months, though the optimism over my adapting to three legs wasn't destined to last. I could now feel new needles of pain throbbing in my good back leg, but did my best to fight through it, since the longer I could make myself last, the happier everyone would be. Pat had taught me well in this. That's the thing about life that can be sort of frustrating—it can keep us around longer than need be.

I wasn't complaining though. Sticking around had some enormous benefits. Not only did I get to see my pups grow even bigger, and our newborn swell even more inside of Kristina, I got to hear some more great music. My buddy Dana Lyons would come over to strum his guitar and cheer me up with his funny song about free-roving bovine revolutionaries.

I think this was Pat's favorite song, and I could almost hear Pat's belly laugh as it was playing. Sometimes Dana would just scratch my ears and that was enough for me.

Swil Kanim, another music budd, would also come over to play violin for both Bernice and me. His stunning notes warmed our house, and seemed to hang in the air long after he stopped playing and had gone home. I felt as if his songs were written just for me.

Swil Kanim started out sort of like me, taken from his family at an early age and put in a foster home. Unlike the people at The Humane Society who truly did care for me, he didn't feel that same sort of love and began playing the violin as a way of expressing his pain and sorrow. He always told my family that we need to make the pain of our lives worthwhile for others. Now that I was veering downhill, I understood this message. My buddy Mitch who works on saving the wilderness for dogs like me stopped by to scratch my ears, but I wished Greg Brown could have stopped by, too. I imagine he was out on tour. Maybe he'd written a song about me.

One morning as I heard Tim stirring, I tried to struggle to my feet in anticipation of my meal when I buckled under the stabbing waves of pain shooting up my one back leg and into my hip. Not a good sign. I fell back onto my bed and tried again this time with a little more success. They had now moved me into the carpeted living room so I wouldn't have to hobble on slippery floors and risk another fall. I gimped over to my food dish and, in my usual fashion, wolfed down my food. I wanted to linger by the bowl in hopes of more, and wouldn't you know it, he dumped an extra scoop in. Now he was getting some of last night's chicken dinner out, and suddenly I was having my second course. I inhaled it in a few breaths, and this seemed to make Tim feel a little better.

After this, they began bringing food right to my bed. What service! The kids seemed to want to stay with me all the time, never wanting to leave my side, even to the point of sleeping with me! I welcomed the attention. I would bark just once when there was a knock at the door, but this was about all I could do. I hardly felt like the protector of my pack and it was sort of frustrating.

faith

It seems like just yesterday that I was a pup. Now I find myself thinking of old Sid back in my early days and I wonder if he's having the last laugh. I now understand his expression that once seemed to say, "Live it up, puppy; you'll be old like me someday." I never thought that day would come, no less so soon. When I was young, I thought I'd be that way forever, strong and bold enough to take on anything. Now I'm not so sure.

I know Oliver will come, too. I feel him not too far away, and boy, are they going to laugh when they see what he looks like. He won't come as a replacement for me, as there will never again be an Ivan like me in the world. That won't be his purpose anyway. His purpose will be to continue the work that I started, and to love, guide, and protect my family and the new pup when she comes. He won't be fierce like me though he'll think that he is, and he'll remain a puppy far longer than I did. He will also sing and howl whenever someone is playing the piano, though he won't have the same appetite for food that I've had. He'll also chase Boris whenever he gets that sneaky cat outside. I do hope he's smarter than I was about love, and that he doesn't cost my family as much as I did.

Tolstoy's great essay entitled "A Confession" has inspired me to speak the truth and learn from it throughout my life. I must confess that even though I'm not the greatest looking dog in the world, I'm fine with who I am, even if others aren't. There will always be dogs and people who won't like you for your looks, but those who judge others are probably a waste of time.

Tolstoy says that we need to sift away all that is not gold in our lives to find the true gold. He says that even though we fail, and will continue to fail, it is our duty to live out these principles to the best of our abilities and to live by faith and reason.

Some people and dogs lack faith, or believe that faith is found by following the paths of others. Really, faith is about creating your own tracks, like a wolf's across an unbroken expanse of snow, believing that as you trudge through, you will find your way. If you plunge into those untouched reaches of lonely white wilderness before you, your guide may appear, a canine friend at your side, ready to go there with you wherever you make your trail. Maybe he won't have all four legs and two eyes, but it won't matter. If you really learn to see, you won't even need your eyes.

good ivan, bad kitty

More old friends have been stopping by as of late and it's been good to see them. The recent trips to visit Colleen at work have been challenging, but it was good to see everyone there too. Apparently the chemotherapy didn't work, and I suspected as much since I've been losing the strength in the other back leg and the pain is getting worse. What a blessing though. Imagine if we all lived for thousands of years how much we might take for granted.

I saw Boris do something the other day which was appalling! He never would have pulled this stunt had I been in my prime but, knowing that I was bed-bound, he sauntered over to the kitchen table where Bernice was enjoying a bowl of soup and, without hesitation, he jumped up onto the table and began slurping soup out of her bowl even while she was eating it! I growled and tried to bark. He just turned at me, eyes gleaming, as if to say, "This is payback for those cheese bricks!" He knew Bernice was so blind and deaf that she couldn't see or hear him, and even if she had, it probably wouldn't have mattered. "Fiend," I whispered, and I know he heard me, though he pretended not to. Boris . . . always looking out for himself.

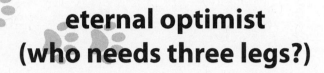

eternal optimist
(who needs three legs?)

It's getting a little embarrassing now that I can't use my other back leg. My family takes turns walking me around the field, holding up my rear in a sling. What a sight I must be to look at. Obviously, cosmetic appearances have never been my primary strength in life, but this is ridiculous. On the other hand, or paw, it somehow seems fitting for a lumpy-headed, one-eyed, underbitten dog with a snaggletooth to be down to his two front legs. Life is good.

I have come to the conclusion that having two legs is not so bad, but if I get down to one, we may have a little problem.

the answer

They're now bringing me great quantities of meat, fish, and other delights, but the strangest thing is I'm not really hungry anymore. I'm almost ashamed as I nudge the pile of food with my nose, attempting to inhale some with a few halfhearted bites. Why couldn't they have done this years ago?

Now, with everybody surrounding me, I'm living in a moment that feels familiar—as they call me by name, I become ever more grateful for having been given one. Over the course of my life, I've been rescued again and again, but now I see that I've been rescued from the worst thing of all—loneliness. The gray dusk that had been slowly consuming me for weeks has changed. How strange. What had first appeared as darkness is now a strange new light and a wondrous new strength is building in me.

In fact, there is a light about everything. All the people who have been coming by glow in the most beautiful way, sort of like an early winter sunlight reflecting off of the snow just before it turns evening pink as it nears the horizon. Or maybe like a late afternoon light that shines after a storm when the sky is still purple with clouds. That kind of light. This feeling isn't new but the only times I remember this light from before were when Tim, Pat, and I stood in the river on that sunny fall day long ago, and once on Goat Mountain as I leaned into a stiff breeze howling about my ears as the sun hung in the west. It's as if I've always been suspended in this very moment, and now I realize that I won't even need my two legs much longer.

The feeling is akin to floating on gentle, rolling waves, only the waves beneath me are waves of love that gently rock me and calm my failing body.

As I lie here, Tim is holding an old American literature anthology from his college days, reading aloud a poem to my beautiful goddess, when suddenly, it happens! Out of nowhere comes the answer to my great question of questions! What is my nature? Bits and pieces have been revealed to me over the course of my life through a series of lessons, but now, when I least expect it, it happens! Understanding! Maybe that's just the poetry of life at work, or maybe it's just fate. All I know is that I have one person to thank for it and for once in my life it's not Kristina . . .

thanks, emily

My nature is love! It's that simple. Out of all the great literature and poetry in the history of the world, Emily Dickinson explained it to me in a line from her simple poem called "Unable Are the Loved to Die," and when I heard it, I wanted to bark with joy!

Emily says, "Unable are the loved to die, for love is immortality." That's it! The question of my nature has been answered! I wouldn't know what it is to be loved if my nature weren't love itself. I have been loved and am thus immortal. How could the knowledge of something so simple yet profound have eluded me for so long? Death, where is thy sting? I see now that every event in my life, every mistake I've ever made, and every lesson learned has prepared me for this one moment of understanding.

Everything has been a blessing.
Now I am complete.
Howlelujah.